WHEN IT MATTERS MOST

Keven Fletcher

Copyright © 2016

Editorial Work by Dave Troesh and AnnaMarie McHargue

Cover Design by Arthur Cherry

Author Photo by Jennifer Fletcher

Interior Design by Aaron Snethen

Published in Boise, Idaho by Elevate Fiction, a division of Elevate Publishing.

Web: www.elevatepub.com

For information please email info@elevatepub.com

ISBN (print): 9781943425327

ISBN (e-book): 9781943425655

Library of Congress: 2015956309

All rights reserved. No portion of this book may be reproduced, stored in a retrieval system, or transmitted in any form or by any means © electronic, mechanical, photocopy, recording, scanning, or other © except for brief quotations in critical reviews or articles, without the prior written permission of the publisher.

Printed in the United States of America.

ENDORSEMENTS

"*When It Matters Most* is a rare achievement. Keven Fletcher creatively weaves a quilt of traditional stories and tales into an inspirational and united opus of learning, love, and life. A true treat to read."

Dan Pontefract
Author of *The Purpose Effect* and *Flat Army*
Chief Envisioner, TELUS

"If there were a genre beyond 'self-help,' that's the aisle where *When It Matters Most* should be found. Keven Fletcher masterfully weaves a set of traditional stories into a single narrative of human connection – with self, with others, with the universe. Though the tales tap insights from across ages and continents, the deep wisdom that unifies this short gem is the most compelling of all."

David Streight
Author of *Breaking into the Heart of Character* and
Interfaith Understanding (with Michele Israel)
Former Executive Director, Center for Spiritual and Ethical Education

"As a busy corporate executive and working mother, I loved reading *When It Matters Most*. It made me pause and deeply reflect on the things that most matter in one's life. It also reminded me to be mindful about the personal narratives I attribute to colleagues or friends and to truly look at who they are rather than my perception of who they are."

Katherine Tweedie
Executive Director, Investec Investment Institute
Former Director and Head of Africa, World Economic Forum

"Mystical, intriguing and like a wise friend you'll always want to draw on – in good times and bad – *When It Matters Most* offers gentle guidance, subtle humor, a shoulder to cry on, and a reminder of what really matters."

Peter Johnston
Author, *Negotiating with Giants*
Corporate and Government Adviser; Managing Director, NAI

"Immensely recognizable, stirring, and comforting, *When It Matters Most* is the gift of having one's own Ghost of Christmas Present, offering wisdom without judgement. A beautiful story that will resonate with anyone, no matter their stage of life, it reminds us how to engage with the world in a way that brings out the beauty in our everyday."

Danielle Ward
Senior Consultant, Holker Watkin Limited

"Although rooted in the ancient and timeless wisdom stories from the world's major religions, *When it Matters Most* will seem familiar to a great many readers. In this well-crafted novel, the main characters evoke admiration, pity, reverence, laughter, and compassion as we watch them engage with the everyday struggles of family, work, addictions, grief, and the desire – often latent – for a connection to some larger community. This book will appeal to readers with an interest in matters both mundane and mystical."

Paul Bramadat
Author of *Spirituality in Hospice Palliative Care* (with Harold Coward)
Director, Centre for Studies in Religion and Society, University of Victoria

"In times of grief and loss, it can be easy to lose the thread of our story, to lose our way. Storytelling can be a bridge to healing, revaluing and the embracing of new possibilities in our life. Elegant and powerful, *When It Matters Most*, is one such bridge."

Dawn Schell
CCC Counselor, University of Victoria

"A cynical, whiskey-drinking Simon grapples with the meaning of life in this suspenseful, mysterious novel. Through his struggles in *When It Matters Most*, we're reminded that everyone has a story and we should take nothing for granted. Extraordinary and delightful."

Chris Considine, QC
Lawyer, Special Prosecutor
Honorable Consul General of Nepal

"Through fourteen beautifully contextualized wisdom tales, *When It Matters Most* drew me to reflect on my own life and experiences. This charming book affirms how what we truly need often presents itself through the most unlikely sources – if we are only open to it."

Susan Haddon
Board Chair, Our Place Society (an outreach to the community's most vulnerable citizens)

"*When it Matters Most* offers very simple yet fulfilling answers to some of the biggest fears that millennials feel today: loneliness, anxiety, pessimism about the future. For all of us preoccupied with seeking success at whatever the cost, the stories from this short novel present another perspective on the life values that we should subscribe to. These are the stories that I want to pass down to my children one day."

Tom Macintosh Zheng
LL.B. Candidate – King's College London
Entrepreneur

"The search for meaning in life, or for a life of meaning, is a universal human journey. Keven Fletcher's unique method of forming a narrative around stories of wisdom begin to shed some light on that path. Once you start reading, you won't be able to sleep until you've finished the last story. Sleep consolidates learning: You will wake up wiser the next day."

JoAnn Deak
Author of *The Driver's Manual for Your Adolescent Brain* and *Your Fantastic Elastic Brain*
Psychologist, Educator, Speaker; The Deak Group

"With a charming, anecdotal tone that inspires us to live our lives full of joy instead of judgement, hope instead of fear, and above all, reverence for our fellow people journeying through life together, *When it Matters Most* greets death with life's greatest questions, "What will my life mean, how will I be remembered, and what really matters?"

Emily Reid
Writer of *Drifter*
Musician/Song Writer at BMG Music

Here's to seizing a meaningful life! Kev

AUTHOR'S NOTE

Most of the characters with whom Simon interacts are amalgams of actual people and events, not intended to represent a particular individual. Where a character has been intentionally and significantly modeled on a single person, I have received permission and extend my gratitude to each of the families involved.

A general word of thanks is offered to all who shared feedback, whether on the concept or the manuscript. Particular recognition must be given for the moral support of Dean, Michael, and Peter, along with the thoughtful expertise of the good folks at Elevate.

For the way their lives exemplify many of the values at the core of the wisdom stories, I also want to thank Marion and Noel.

The book is dedicated to my spouse, Jenn, and daughter, Kaeleigh, both of whom can be glimpsed throughout the text by those who know them. Their presence reflects how they continuously inspire and enrich my experience of life beyond these pages.

CHAPTER ONE

Simon already savors the praise that will come. The flow had been seamless, the content uplifting and poignant. People had laughed. People had cried. They endured their brush with mortality and it hadn't been that bad.

Concluding the benediction, Simon motions for the congregation to be seated. As one, they ease into straight-backed pews. Stepping out from the pulpit, his black robes and white stole sway as he descends the four steps to the congregation. His manner exudes authority, absolute control of the moment.

He approaches the deceased's family, neatly displayed in the front pew. Moving from relative to relative, he shakes their hands and offers each some word of comfort. The nephew who offered part of the eulogy is thanked for his thoughts, so well chosen. The young cousin who sang a solo is told how much her voice added to the service, setting the tone. The sister who was in tears, Simon crouches so that their faces are level and softly holds her hand for a moment between his own, no words. He continues through the others, delivering efficiently scripted blessings – the fruit of 29 years as a minister.

Stepping back and lifting his arms, Simon signals for the congregation to rise and then silently invites the family to leave. Stoic, they exit the sanctuary, making their way down the long corridor to the reception hall. Simon follows, but leaves the procession midstream, sidestepping into his office. Pulling the door closed behind him, he tests the latch and draws the blind over its small window. Time for a last ritual. His personal Amen.

Simon has no problem standing before crowds, but dislikes being in them. He attributes this aversion to having little use for small talk.

Reaching behind the stoles in his closet, he pulls out a bottle of Edradour. Viewing the scotch at arm's length, he resolves that the service was, after all, a special occasion. He pours a shot, replaces the bottle, adjusts his robe, and settles into his chair. The first sip burns agreeably.

Reviewing his performance, Simon deems the service a success. His eulogy was accented by the knowing nods of the congregation. The final prayer tied the deceased's life together in a neat package. The organist had been a little slow, but what could one expect? He would remind her next time. Pacing is everything.

Then came the knock. Draining the glass, suppressing the cough, Simon rises and opens the door.

She stands about 5 foot, 2 inches and couldn't be more than twelve, thirteen at most. A soft smile greets him. Disheveled chestnut hair not quite past her shoulders, she wears a cranberry turtleneck and a black, ankle length skirt. Hazel eyes.

As she surveys the office, Simon follows her gaze. His desk is in its usual disarray, books and paper strewn across the top and onto a side table. The ficus shows signs of neglect. One wall is covered floor-to-ceiling with bookshelves, not a volume's width unoccupied. The other walls display art: a Vickers print of a church in Kitkatlit, framed pages from a medieval prayer book, favored works in crayon by children of the church. A small coffee table is centered between four, well-worn leather armchairs.

Taking in the room, the child nods thoughtfully. There's no awkwardness about her. No sign of hesitation or hurry.

Simon breaks the silence, "What can I do for you?" Not that he wants to do anything for her. At least, not just after a service. This was his time to make the adjustment between the formal liturgy and the informal crowd. Eight minutes was all it took. Eight minutes of uninterrupted peace. She closes the door, reopens the blind, and flops down in a chair, his chair. Each of the four is identical to the others, yet Simon prefers the position of one.

From that chair she asks, "What do you think of her?"

Several thoughts pass through Simon's mind, the predominant being his distaste for this rather impertinent youth, breezing into his office, taking his chair. Normally, he would politely suggest that they join the reception, but her question catches him off guard, "What do I think of whom?"

"The person that died." Her tone subtly shifts, "The service was about Sandra, wasn't it? You gave most of the eulogy. What do you think of her?"

Adult to child, he corrects, "What *did* I think of her."

Her smile broadens. With arms on the rests, she's clearly at home and not about to leave. She examines Simon's expression and motions to the chair across from her own, "Take a seat and tell me about her."

Surprised by his compliance, Simon assures himself that he's doing so out of pastoral concern. Like others who lose a loved one to whom they weren't particularly close, the girl wants to know more.

He thinks back to when he first learned about Sandra, searching for an anecdote he might offer.

Like so many funerals, I didn't know the deceased. There was a time, of course, when most everyone was connected to a church. Now it's often the case that those few who do enter the doors arrive to get married, baptize their children, and be buried. The first two events are often out of order. The third is out of their control.

So my introduction to Sandra comes in the form of a voice on the phone requesting that I meet with her nephew. The next day I find myself sitting in an architect's office, pen in hand, hoping to hear something remotely personal that I can relate about his aunt.

I already knew that Sandra had made it to the age of 83, which is good news. It means I can say that she had "a long and full life." More than any prayer or ritual, it's this little phrase that brings comfort to mourners. You can feel the transformation. Crying eyes are reduced to dabbed tears. Tentative smiles of recognition creep across nervous faces. Its effect is constant, regardless of the truth. Not surprisingly, it works when applied to octogenarians who lived generous and full lives. That it works equally well with those who were absolute bastards, living out their emptiness over decades, never ceases to amuse me. But loved or despised, it's all the same. Mourners want to know that as far as deaths go, this was a reasonable one…and theirs will be as well.

"Tell me about your aunt."

The nephew places a photograph album before me. As I turn the pages, I notice that the corners of the black matt sheets are shiny from the gentle wear of fingertips. This album had not been created and abandoned on a bookshelf. It had been carefully compiled over the course of decades and visited regularly.

"It was hers," he states, staring at the album, his own age marked by wisps of grey hair. He's meticulously dressed, as well presented as the drawings that line the walls.

The pages of Sandra's childhood and youth are typical. Sitting in a bucket of water on a blazing day. Riding a pony, its lead rope running horizontally out of the frame. Smiling, blowing out candles. The pictures are vibrant moments stilled in a mix of greys.

Then a few pages later, she's a stunning young woman. I pause. She's roughly eighteen, diving off a three-meter cliff into a lake – a black, one-piece bathing suit set against her pale skin. The angle of the shot suggests that the photographer was in a boat, looking upwards. The shutter snaps the moment after she pushes far off the cliff in a perfect swan dive. Arms stretched. Back arched. Eyes open. Fearless.

And posed. With manual film cameras, it's one thing to get the right combination of aperture and shutter that matches your film speed on the first try. It's another to do so for a moving object. Add the complexity of shooting from a boat, no matter how calm the day, and you can easily blow through a roll or two to get such a perfect shot. I imagine her swimming to the surface and over to the boat, smiling as she's waved on by her friend to try the dive again and again. The hidden process intrigues me more than the flawless result.

Turn the page. She's twenty and seated at a round bar table with a small candle at its center. Although she's alone in the shot, the other seats await the return of her friends, half-consumed drinks in place. Sandra eyes the camera, feigning displeasure. Her legs are tightly crossed. The swirl of smoke remains even as she holds the cigarette away from her face. More than beauty, she exudes strength. Again, there's something very intentional about the shot. She's more than posed, she's positioned.

I get the feeling that I've lingered a little long over these pictures and move to the next page, looking for a way to re-engage the nephew.

Sandra's now 25 and somehow different. I flip back to the previous page. It's her eyes. "Yes," says the nephew, as if waiting for me to notice. "That's Sandra-After. She was beautiful, athletic, smart, ambitious and then...not. Before and after, like someone flipped a switch."

The next pages are filled mostly with photographs of other people, not Sandra. Other people and jigsaw puzzles.

The people, I'm told, were patients and staff from the care homes. In her affections, Sandra did not distinguish between the two. Meanwhile, the puzzles became her passion. After mastering the 500 piece, basic sets that depicted buildings and mountains, she ultimately moved on to the 1000+ puzzles with uniform pieces that created abstract designs.

Taking a closer look at the photos, it seems clear that these projects were a social act, drawing others into her world. Most of the shots were taken by her, but even when in the frame, she was hardly ever alone. The final picture captures Sandra at a dining table with a friend on either side. Her companions are engrossed in the puzzle, but Sandra is smiling at the camera, puzzle piece in hand. It's a beautiful shot, though in tone it couldn't be more different from the earlier ones.

"What happened?"

"She developed schizophrenia in her early twenties. Sandra excelled academically, and socially for that matter. She was on her way to becoming a lawyer. Six months after the diagnosis, she was out of school. In two years, she was living in a home. We were all so disappointed for her." The nephew pauses before adding, "When you offer the eulogy, the family would like you to concentrate on Sandra-Before."

―――

Which is exactly what Simon did, other than the mandatory recognition of her age.

A voice breaks into his thoughts. "So you wrote her off as a duster, like she sat in her chair and nothing happened for the last sixty years?"

Abruptly shifting to the present, Simon's back with his young visitor. "No, I wouldn't say that nothing happened. There's every indication that she was loved by her friends and the staff." Thinking of the thumb-worn corners, he adds, "and she loved them back. She was fond of revisiting her moments with them."

The girl nods. Simon senses agreement, not approval.

She leans forward, "Where was that in your service? No mention of a tight squad in the care home. You left us thinking that she might as well have died in her twenties."

Flustered, Simon scrambles for a defense, "Sandra developed schizophrenia. Would you have me celebrate her illness?" He expects the answer that will allow him to end the conversation and send the unusual child on her way.

"Better than an answer," the girl eases back into her seat, "I've got a story for you."

―――

Once, there were two friends on a journey. Despite an already long day on their horses, they push themselves and their beasts to reach the next gated town before nightfall. The road they traveled was known for its bandits and they didn't want to be caught out on their own after dark.

Just as the sun slips over the horizon, they see a town in the distance. When they arrive, they knock on the gate.

A voice rises from behind the wall, "The gate is closed for the evening. Come back tomorrow."

"Please," protests the first friend, "we've been traveling all day and could use some food and a warm bed."

"The gate is closed. Come back tomorrow."

"You must understand," continues the first friend, "there are bandits on this road and without the protection of your walls, we are in danger."

"How do we know that you're not the bandits? The gate is closed. Come back tomorrow."

As the two men walk their horses back from the gate, the first friend despairs, "Can you believe our luck? After traveling all day, we must have missed the gate by a matter of minutes. Look at those clouds. What if it rains? This is terrible."

"Well," says the second, "who knows, maybe it's terrible and maybe it's not. Let's find a place to camp."

So the men get back on their horses and find a clearing beside the road that they passed earlier in the day. They settle their horses and build a fire. Comforted by its warmth, they begin to cook their food. At that moment, the clouds open and it begins to pour. The fire goes out and the men are drenched. They gather their belongings and move farther from the road, hoping to find some protection from the rain by clinging to the hillside.

As they walk their horses, the first friend says, "You know, it was bad enough to not get into the town, but now we're soaked and our dinner is ruined. How terrible."

"Well," says the second, "who knows, maybe it's terrible and maybe it's not. Let's see if we can find some shelter."

The first friend is about to tell the second what he might do with that shelter, when they happen upon a cave. Glad to be out of the weather, the men leave their horses by the entrance and go inside. It's deeper than they wish to go without a torch. Happily, there's plenty of room for them both at the front. Lying on the ground, but covered by dry blankets from their saddlebags, the men are about to fall asleep, when they hear a roar from the back of the cave. The horses spook and gallop away. The friends run for their lives and quickly climb a tree.

"Unbelievable," exclaims the first. "What are the chances of so many things going wrong? We have no luck at all. Our horses are gone. The rain is falling so hard that I can hardly hear myself think. This is terrible."

"Well," says the second, "who knows, maybe it's terrible and maybe..." One look from his friend makes it clear that he better not finish the sentence.

Afforded a view from the trees, the men see a collection of torchlights moving swiftly along the road. "Such a large party. It must be a dignitary," posits the second friend.

"And if it's a dignitary," continues the first, "they will certainly open the gate for him."

With that, the two men scramble down their tree and run for the road. They emerge from the bushes at its edge, shouting and waving their arms just as the party gallops past. Because of the rain and the darkness, they go unnoticed.

"What do you have to say to that?" asks the first friend. "Any pithy words of wisdom to offer?"

"Well," says the second, "I still say, who knows? We might as well start walking for town. By the time we arrive, the sun will be up."

Several hours of silence later, the two men arrive at the gates, one of which is ripped from its hinges. They enter to find burnt buildings and the town turned upside down. Most of those finding their way through the wreckage are very old or very young. A woman tells them, "The bandits came in the middle of the night, broke through the gate, stole from our homes, and took many of our people as slaves."

After spending a week at the village, helping wherever they could, the two friends take their leave. When the town drops from sight, the first friend turns to the second, "If the guard had let us in that night, we would have been taken as slaves with the townspeople. If the rain had not come, dousing our fire and driving us to seek shelter away from the road, we would have been seen by the bandits as they passed. If we had succeeded in getting back to the road in time to wave down the party, they would have taken us then. All these things I thought were terrible...in the end, they kept us safe."

The second smiles, "Which is why, my friend, whenever something out of my control seems bad, I try to withhold judgment. I remind myself out loud: Maybe it's terrible and maybe it's not – who knows?"

For Simon, the silence that follows is full. The muffled chatter of a hundred mourners seeps through the office door. The girl continues to look straight at him, even after he drops his gaze.

Her voice is steady. "Try this thought: Sandra suffered an illness that changed the course of her life, sure; she looked like she was heading for a certain kind of success and that was lost, sure." Simon's eyes meet hers as she continues, "But that's not the only kind of success. You've already said that Sandra had people she loved who loved her back and I can tell you that she was thankful for every year of her life.

Yet, somehow to you her last sixty were so terrible they shouldn't be mentioned." A brief pause, her words gathering weight, "Before you start editing other people's stories, Simon, maybe you should figure out whether your own is worth telling."

The girl rises from her chair, walks to the door and turns the knob before Simon reacts. Jumping to his feet, he asks, "How do you know how Sandra felt?"

She casts a smile over her shoulder, "Another day," and clicks the door shut behind her. Simon stands dumbfounded, then slumps back into the chair across from his own.

CHAPTER TWO

Swallowing a mouthful of tea, she postulates, "It might only be us."

I find it strange, the idea of Shen's funeral consisting of only this sister, their father and those paid to attend.

Statuesque and dressed in fashionable casuals, she continues, "I don't know what Shen was doing over the last twenty years." Another mouthful. "I guess I got tired of being my brother's keeper." She pauses to ensure that I've captured her little joke. A rather glib reference given the situation, but a returned smile keeps her happy.

My host sits on an amply stuffed, leather couch. Her father and I sit across from her on its exact twin. The apartment is well appointed with polished furniture, precise accent lighting, and plants of unnatural health. A brilliantly colorful abstract commands the wall over the fireplace.

I wonder how the aesthetics compare to the apartment where her brother cracked his skull tumbling down a concrete staircase. Ill-timed haste coupled with excessive consumption, he died at forty-seven an impoverished alcoholic. Perhaps no one could keep Shen, let alone save him, but the sister's grin escapes me.

At the distant end of the couch, the father stares into his cup, holding it with both hands, rubbing his right thumb side to side across its rim. At some point I'll offer a reassuring word about his wife now having company on the other side. Either that or a simple recognition that children should never die before their parents. Neither will actually impact his grief, but I'm expected to say something that sounds as if it might help. At the very least, a reassuring phrase cleanly draws these meetings to an orderly end.

Back to the present moment, I pick up the last strand and regroup, "So, you're thinking that the service will only consist of ourselves and the funeral director?"

"Probably. But I did put an obituary in the paper. If he had friends, it's possible that a few of them will see it. That's why I thought I'd prepare a few words about Shen, you know, from happier times."

I look for his father's response. He slowly nods his head, cradling his cup.

"That would be nice," I say, and not only for those in attendance. The sister's offer cuts my work in half. Funerals are a good sideline for any minister. All the pay and a fifth of the hassle associated with weddings. If someone took the eulogy, even better, especially in the case of a tragic circumstance.

Not the accident itself, mind you. People die in accidents all the time. The tragedy lay in how Shen lived his life. More to the point, how he wasted it. Finding the right words to positively spin a life like his devours time and creative energy.

I pursue the advantage, "If others do come, would you like them to share a few words as well?"

"Sure, maybe we'll find out what he's been up to." Another smile. This time the father offers no response. His thumb has stopped wearing its path. The meeting isn't over, but he's already left. I warmly shake his hand, but save my words of comfort for when they can be heard.

———

Simon arrives at the funeral home 45 minutes early. Prompt, not for the sake of the dead, but more for relishing a moment of peace before dealing with the living. The clergy office in this funeral home is much the same as every other. The room is cramped. The desk is small. Two hooks for robes hang in the corner by the mirror and clock. A short bookcase holds a collection of hymnals, bibles, and volumes of poetry

— last ditch resources for the unprepared. A box of tissues stands ready for the sentimental.

Robe over arm, Simon drops his folder on the corner of the desk before finding one of the hooks.

Centered on the table is an envelope. Simon reaches for it. Enclosed is a generic note of thanks from the funeral director, a copy of Shen's obituary, and the check. He scrutinizes the amount before folding it into his wallet.

Simon removes his robe from the hook and enwraps himself. Following routine, he turns to the mirror and watches himself as if a third party. His hands grasp the long, narrow stole at midpoint, raising it to his lips for the kiss. He lifts it over his head, carefully setting it across the back of his neck and over his shoulders. The mirror follows his fingers as they dutifully straighten the ensemble.

Checking the folds once more, he catches his own eye. Satisfied with the transformation, Simon picks up his folder and opens the door, which is blocked by another minister.

Simon notes the man's somewhat threadbare robe, along with his short stature and strikingly vigorous mustache. Without thought, Simon steps back and feigns an apology. The minister enters the room, blocking Simon from the door before turning his back to take advantage of the mirror. He starts to fuss with his clerical collar, which refuses to rest squarely in place.

Simon expands his apology, "Oh, so sorry. You need the room. I didn't realize there was another service."

"There isn't."

"Pardon?"

"Yours is the only one this afternoon."

"Then you're meeting with a family?"

"No," the minister abandons his collar and turns, "I'm waiting for you."

As a rule, Simon finds his colleagues irritating. For reasons he finds obvious, he places responsibility for his negative conception at their feet. Between the robe, the mustache, and the obtuse behavior, little about this particular minister suggests a challenge to his understanding. The word, flake, pops into Simon's mind.

"Look, we don't have a lot of time today," the minister presses. "Tell me what you know about Shen."

"You're quite right; I have a service to lead." Simon feels his diagnosis confirmed, so he takes charge, "What's this about?"

"Tell me what you know about the man."

"See here, Padre," disdainful, Simon straightens and leans slightly forward, "I don't know who you are. If you want to know about Shen, stay for the service, but I've got to be going. Goodbye."

As Simon brushes past, the minister gently places a hand on Simon's shoulder and asserts unhurriedly, "You think you know his value, but you don't."

"And I suppose you're going to enlighten me?"

"My dear Simon, you have no idea." Under the mustache, a smile spreads, "But this is Shen's day and there's still plenty of time for a story. I suggest we take a seat."

The young man sits across from the old woman, tears welling in his eyes. The words leave his lips as a confession, "I'm worthless."

She pours out two cups of tea, careful to first waken the dry leaves with a splash of hot water before allowing them to steep. They open to the warmth of the liquid, now infused with a pale green. Each cup receiving precise attention, time passes before she speaks.

"Who has told you this?"

"My father and mother. I'm not following the path they would have me walk."

The woman places one of the cups before the young man and gestures that he drink. His hands tremble as he blows across the cup before taking a quick sip. The old woman smiles. She takes her cup, wrapping both hands around its warmth. She brings it to her face. Instead of exhaling, she draws in a long, slow breath through her nostrils, savoring the aroma. Without drinking, she sets down her cup.

"And their opinion leaves you without value?"

Her pace influences his own. The young man takes a whiff of the tea before sipping. The torrent of emotion lessens, "They are my parents. They have done so much for me and I love them." He pauses, "But this time I cannot do what they ask of me."

She nods. Her eyes hold no judgement, neither agreeing nor disagreeing. The young man relaxes. Taking the cup in her hands, raising it to her face, the woman again draws in the aroma, then drinks. She repeats the process a second time before returning her cup to the table.

Pulling a simple ring from her weathered finger, she hands it to the young man, "Take this ring to the merchants in the marketplace. See what they offer for it, then return to me."

Uncertain, but not wanting to offend, the young man leaves the woman to her tea and makes his way to the marketplace. He first approaches the bread maker, who feels the weight of the ring in his hand and makes an offer. Next, he seeks out the butcher, who holds the ring so that it catches the light and reveals its sheen before she makes a bid. From merchant to merchant he travels, until finally he reaches the knife maker, who checks the inside of the ring for markings and names a price.

Returning to the old woman, he retakes his seat. She asks, "Do you know the value of my ring?" The young man recounts his conversations with the merchants in the market and the range of their offers. "Now," the woman responds, "please take my ring to the jeweler at the edge of town."

Again, wanting to assist the old woman, the young man walks to the outskirts of town. The jeweler opens his door and takes the ring into his shop. Affixing his loupe, he inspects the ring and places it on a scale. He says that it's a rare find, that he's only seen two that were similar. He names a price ten times the highest bid of the merchants.

Soon the young man sits again with the old woman, who asks, "Now do you know the value of my ring?" He places the ring into her outstretched palm and relates the words of the jeweler, along with the price.

The woman responds by setting the ring on the table between them and prepares two fresh cups of tea. She awakens the leaves, lets them steep, and finally pours. Taking the cups in their hands, they both inhale and savor.

"You see," said the old woman, "the value of my ring varies according to whom you ask. If you let the baker determine its value, it would be low indeed. If you believe the jeweler, its worth is high." She sips her tea and repeats, "So, do you know the value of my ring?"

"The jeweler best knows its worth."

The old woman nods, "It's true that I should listen closely to what the jeweler has to say. It's also true that I should consider what the merchants tell me." She picks up the ring. "Yet, these people cannot determine the value this ring holds for me."

As she holds the ring in her palm, the young man notices the worn mark on the finger where it usually rested. "Ultimately, I determine its worth," she gently nods as she speaks, "just as I must determine my own."

They finish their tea, unrushed.

Story time done, I ask the minister for his name. He says that this isn't about him. It's about Shen and my disposition toward assumptions.

What the hell.

I watch in silence as he walks down the hall and out the exit, then check the clock while gathering my notes. Usually I'd wait for the funeral director to claim me at the last minute. Not today. A public space seems preferable.

Now I face the sister and father with time to spare and must make conversation. I measure my breathing and select from the usual phrases.

While chatting with the sister, I scan the room over her shoulder, looking for the mustache. Of the five people in the small chapel, only one is noteworthy. He looks rough. Not quite like a street person, but bedraggled. His hair is dark, shoulder length, and in need of washing. His beard is unkempt. Even from a distance, his eyes strike me as haunting.

Yet, I'd prefer his company to the minister's. My mind momentarily re-cornered in the office, I barely follow the father's words about a camping trip when the children were young. I pull myself back to the present, noting the influx of additional mourners. "Nice that others have come," I offer, sparking another round of polite conversation.

The flow of arrivals is steady. As usual, the seats in the middle and back fill first, reluctance showing on the faces of those forced to the front. Not expecting a crowd, I hadn't reserved seats for the sister and father. I lay my folder across two seats in the front row. Not proper, but practical. In the background, the director motions that more chairs will be brought. Soon, there's no more room for sitting and bodies accumulate against the back wall.

Thankfully, people are always patient at funerals. Doesn't matter how disorganized the directors or how long the speakers, the presence of a corpse commands perspective. A funeral may cause you to be uncomfortable, bored, or late for the rest of your day, but at least you're outside the box.

The sister turns and surveys the crowd. She holds her folder with one hand as the other fidgets with the papers inside. I'd feel a little unnerved in her shoes. It's one thing for the hired collar to not know much about the deceased. It's another for a sister to know less than her growing audience.

I take a final look around the room. No mustache. I signal the start.

When it comes time for the eulogy, the sister pulls out her notes, assembles them on the lectern and recounts some of Shen's childhood exploits: the pinecones thrown from the uppermost branches of an impossibly tall tree, the retaliatory sand sprinkled on a neighbor's freshly painted windowsill, the late night debates fueled by first year philosophy classes. It dawns on me that the siblings were once quite close. Her comments end with a story about her brother's twenty-fifth birthday. She pauses, seems to gather herself to say something more, then shakes her head ever so slightly before finding her seat.

I take her place, "Would anyone like to offer a few more words in Shen's memory?"

Nothing.

The stillness that follows is no surprise. More often than not the request is met with silence. It's my job to tough out the uncomfortable quiet, so that a speaker can gather his or her thoughts before stepping to the lectern.

With the seconds ticking along, I offer a knowing smile to those gathered, as if to assure them that I, too, share their sense of discomfort and that our mutual relief will arrive soon enough.

Nothing.

I take one step back from the pulpit and lower my eyes, not wanting to create the appearance of pressure or judgement. I muse that perhaps they're waiting for a written invitation. Raising my eyes, I find myself curious. What do they know about Shen? There's a reason they came, different from that of his sister and father. I allow more room than usual for someone to step forward.

Nothing.

Too uncomfortable. I step forward, raise my eyes to those assembled, open my mouth to offer the closing prayer, when the man with the unsettling eyes clears his throat. I stop, but he doesn't move. Instead, someone from the next row in a dark suit and red tie rises from his seat and makes his way to the front.

Grasping the lectern with both hands, he talks of the time that Shen spent as a high school teacher in his early thirties. How the students sought him out for personal advice. How he could shift the tension in a staff meeting with a subtle joke. How he made people feel valued over the smallest of things.

The speaker stops and takes a breath. His tone shifts. Speaking of alcoholism as if it were a separate entity, an external intrusion, he shares how Shen's demon would take him. Even more concretely, how it stole his friend but didn't negate the good he brought to those around him. Shen would be missed.

As he walks back to his seat, a woman in a modest summer dress steps forward. Her thoughts are punctuated with pauses whenever her voice cracks.

She talks about how Shen came to her workplace as a laborer after his career as a teacher ended. He hadn't been there all that long before she got into a conflict with her boss and lost her job. A few weeks later, Shen called out of the blue and invited her for coffee. They chatted for an hour. When it came time for the two of them to leave, Shen slipped her an envelope with a month's worth of rent, not to be repaid.

The woman scans the congregation, seeking out the red tie. She agrees, Shen did have a demon but it did not define him.

Others come forward to speak. Impressions meld together, joined with a liturgical tag about the reality of the demon and the value of the man. I look down at the front row to the sister and father. They sit side-by-side, eyes straight forward, unfocussed. Having enough trouble unpacking my own thoughts, I don't venture to speculate about theirs. I close the service as quickly as possible, shake an appropriate number of hands, and depart.

Out on the street, a tap on the shoulder from behind interrupts my retreat. No mustache and collar. Instead, it's the haunting eyes. He extends his hand, pulls me slightly forward, and does not let go. "Sometimes," his tone as earnest as his voice hoarse, "Sometimes people's lives get broken into pieces, but that doesn't mean they're not whole."

Thanking me for letting people be honest, he extols my virtues before releasing my hand. As he strides away, my eyes follow him, knowing that his praise is misplaced. At best, I'm one of the merchants, not the old woman.

CHAPTER THREE

"So, who are you planting today?"

Vibrantly blue eyes deliver the grin as she takes another mouthful of breakfast. Simon notes that it's been the same menu for five years and three months. A daughter's quiet tribute to her mother. At age fourteen, Ailish learned how to make the granola at her mother's side, three months before the latter succumbed to cancer. Now, it was like the prophet Elijah had blessed the container in which the granola was kept, never to be empty again. Splashing on the almond milk, each morning became an act of remembrance poured out over cranberries, raisins, apricots, almonds, pecans, pumpkin seeds, coconut, cinnamon, honey, and oats.

Simon takes his daughter's jibe in stride. "Nobody. But I am meeting the family of a recently retired and expired COO." Pulling up a chair to the small table and pouring himself a bowl, he wonders to what degree his daughter prepares the granola to comfort herself or him. An unspoken ritual of their life together, it's an entirely unexplored constant.

"What sort of guy?"

"A Chief Operations Officer," he explains.

"Yah, I get what he did, but what sort of guy was he?"

"Given the waterfront address, a wealthy sort of guy. Beyond that, I guess I'll find out."

"Do you ever get tired of it?"

"Of what?"

"The death thing. You do a lot of funerals."

"You cost a lot of money."

He catches Ailish mid-bite, triggering an indecorous snort. Laughter erupts. Still chortling, she repositions a few of the wilder strands of honey blond hair behind her ear.

Simon's relieved that the previous night's row has faded. He decides to let go of his need for an apology and considers himself gracious for this unspoken gesture, especially given her behavior. In fact, for Simon this moment with Ailish feels like an echo from better times. Not quite the real thing, but better than the alternative. They're both holding on for as long as possible. Two more years of university for her and then – release for them both.

But for now, the simple solace of routine and conversation around a table.

———

Perhaps "wealthy" didn't quite capture this guy. I'm led through the entrance hall and into the dining room. Not so much like mine.

Stunningly elegant, the mission style furniture is something out of a Stickley Catalog, complete with harvest table, inlaid chairs, and dual sideboards. Floor to ceiling windows provide an ocean-view backdrop, balancing the exceptionally large, plaster-framed mirror on the opposite wall. The table is set with myself and five family members: the widow, three adult children, and the deceased's mother.

They're slightly more animated than the furniture.

Usually by this point in the conversation, shared memories stimulate some laughter as family members recount favorite stories. Especially with a parent present, antics from early days are dusted off and displayed for the younger generation. Eyes sparkle with equal parts sorrow and joy, a near universal expression of loss and gratitude.

But not at this table. Not when it comes to my COO. I'm struggling to get them to talk, so I lob a gentle opener, "Tell me about Barry."

The family offers a lot of detail about the deceased's professional life. His upward progression between organizations sounds less like stages in a career and more like the consecration and dissolution of marriages, positioning him as a master of upward mobility through serial polygamy. Clearly, he completely dedicated himself to each company, right until the point when he jumped to the next opportunity. On the way, he fathered special initiatives and took on projects as his darlings, until eventually he retired from a position that accurately reflected his abilities, passions, and aspirations.

What I'm not hearing is very much about his marriage, his children, or the life they shared. I shape my next question more carefully, "When you were growing up, what did Barry like to do with you?"

The eldest relates a time when Barry took on the daily task of driving all three children to school. As the others join in the memory, they focus on his car, a 1983 Maserati Biturbo. Despite its legendary trips to the mechanic, the two-door GT was a particular point of pride for their father. They would cramp together in the back seat, sumptuous upholstery covered to protect against the vagaries of young passengers. At any sign of sunshine, the top would retract, creating such a sense of speed. The black bullet, they called it. When the engine roared, it was awesome. When it didn't, they took mom's Volvo.

When he landed his first COO post, Barry upgraded his ride to the more dependable and sexy BMW Z3, which didn't have a rear seat, but did have the new 2.8 liter engine. I approve of his choice, nodding my head until it occurs to me that this topic is driving the table nowhere near a destination connected to my original question.

Having heard enough about the career and the cars, I try a third time.

"What about Barry as a father – what was he like?"

Taking turns, they present me with a list. He provided a good house, good schools, good vacations, good clothes, good riding stables, good sports camps, good dance classes...

Then the youngest puts an end to it, "He set us up well, but his first love was the office. We didn't see a lot of him on a daily basis."

No one protests. Her words draw a line under the list, nothing more to be added. We move to safer ground, the format of the service and its location. Given the anticipated attendance, the service needs more space than my sanctuary can offer. We talk about the various alternatives and I allow the administrative details to fill the void.

Like the director of a massive production, Simon leads the congregation through Barry's funeral. Christ Church Cathedral provides both the capacity and aesthetics to establish the right tone. Vaulted ceilings and grey stone pillars combine with ornate tapestries and brass ornaments. The massive organ reverberates through every stone and person, drawing the congregation back to another time. The eldest son reads the 23rd Psalm, perhaps the most universally recognizable scripture passage. Two of Barry's colleagues regale the assembled with tales of his work life and golf swing. The soloist both lifts and soothes the four hundred who have gathered, provoking the right amount of tears. Each word of prayer and benediction falls perfectly into place.

All this leaves Simon with every expectation that people will be thrilled with his leadership and they do not disappoint him. The praise at the reception is profuse. People shake his hand and declare that they want him to preside at their funerals. He chuckles agreeably, soaking in their approval.

He remains at the reception for the correct length, the calculation of which has nothing to do with minutes or needs. Over the years he concluded that once half of the attendees depart, it's reasonable that he go as well. The appointed threshold having been crossed, he takes his leave of the family, but not before the eldest son subtly slips him an envelope.

Setting off at a quick pace, robe over his arm, Simon finds himself feeling strangely out of sorts. Instead of the anticipated euphoria, he senses himself deflating. Heading through the downtown core toward his own church, he decides that perhaps it'll be a couple of shots, then home.

Once out of sight of the Cathedral, he opens the envelope and releases a low whistle. Twice the usual amount. Cash.

The whistle echoes. Simon tracks the sound. In the middle of a small green space to the left, a homeless man gestures that there's a spot free on his bench. When it looks like the offer is declined, the man calls, "Simon, take a seat, my friend."

Carefully folding the envelope and placing it securely inside the flap of his jacket, Simon approaches. "Do I know you?"

"You most certainly do. Now take a seat and let's have that drink."

Unprepared, Simon can't hide his unvarnished horror at the thought of sharing a bottle with someone quite this dirty. What phrase did his wife use to describe people in this state? Ridden hard and put away wet – that was it. Yet the sunken eyes and worn face are undeterred.

"Don't be such a prick. It's a fresh bottle and I got you a clean cup from Timmy's. Sit the hell down and tell me about the service."

"Who are you?"

Removing the wrapper, he twists the top and pours the whiskey into a paper cup, "Aren't you getting tired of that question?" He offers it up to Simon.

"Enough. You're connected with the other two, aren't you? What's this about? Who's behind this?"

"Simon, I'll decide my boundaries; you decide yours. You can stay or you can go; it's up to you. But if you stay, make the most of it. Now take a dram or get the hell out of my park."

Eyes lock, seconds pass. Simon reaches for the cup and sits as far along the short bench as possible. More time passes. He takes a sip, along with a few breaths. Nothing unusual happens. Though he still feels unsettled, his shoulders begin to relax; he's not sure why. Simon looks up to the sky, dappled sunlight filtering through the trees. He puts words to his unease.

"The service was perfect, but hollow. Barry never darkened the Cathedral's doors until today. None of his kids wanted to offer the eulogy. His colleagues told stories about his effectiveness at work, not about his work being worthwhile. Even the soloist was nothing more than a paid outsider. Barry looked good and I looked good, but it was a sham."

The homeless man nods and takes a drink from the bottle, "And how does this guy differ from Sandra and Shen? What do you notice?"

"Right. So you are working with the others."

"Don't be boring."

Simon gathers himself, "Seems to me that Barry stands at the other end of the spectrum from Sandra and Shen. They look like lost causes, but their contributions are remarkable. Meanwhile, everything Barry touches turns to gold, but other than the sparkle, his contributions are…unexceptional."

"Good start. Are you ready?"

"You're going to tell a story?"

"It's why I'm here."

―――

Long ago, there lived a Matriarch who ruled over a vast realm. When she began her reign, the region was quite poor and the people suffered from hunger and the cold winter winds.

Out of their need, they turned to each other for comfort, whether it be a warm meal or encouraging word. Under the Matriarch's guidance, the people found that together they could improve their lot. Over time, their stomachs grew fuller and their homes sturdier. They were proud of the life they created side-by-side.

But as time rolls forward, the people become comfortable in their wealth. They no longer need to rely on each other. Even when some fall back into the experience of hunger and cold, others see little reason to disturb their own lives. Instead, the people of the realm are seized with the idea of scarcity; they need to protect what is theirs. At this point, the people begin again to suffer, not from the poverty of hunger or cold, but from a poverty of heart and spirit. Perhaps most sadly of all, the people do not see what they have become.

Fortunately, the Matriarch understands the danger and decides to act.

She sends her couriers to the corners of the realm, inviting all of her citizens to join in a banquet, hosted in the city square. They tell of a gathering with great food and music and dance. The only entrance requirement is a bottle of the region's wine to be poured into a communal bowl and then distributed and consumed together. The food and entertainment will be a gift from the Matriarch.

As the date of the banquet approaches, excitement grows. The citizens speculate about what rare treats will be served, what music will be played. Perhaps there will be fireworks or magic acts. As the day approaches, cellars open and bottles of wine are readied.

Entering the packed square, all is beyond expectation. Their senses are greeted by music and magic. In the center stands an immense bowl. Into this font, each citizen pours a bottle of wine.

After a marvelous dinner, the crowd is silenced by a spray of fireworks.

The Matriarch calls for everyone to fill their goblets from the font. With the last glass charged, they raise them together, salute their land, and drink.

Silence. Then murmurs. The wine is awful. Undrinkable.

The Matriarch calls to the crowd, "My people, I give you the taste of who we have become. You must decide who we will be." With these words, she leaves.

The people are dumbfounded. Why would the Matriarch taint the wine they brought? What did she mean by it being the taste of who they'd become?

It starts with an old man, who stands in front of the crowd, "I thought with so many people contributing wine, I didn't need to bring my best. I brought a lesser bottle. The fault for the taste is mine." The man's honesty frees others to admit that they did the same. Still others confess that under similar reasoning, they topped up half of their bottles with water. A few share that they didn't bother putting any wine in their bottles, a little juice to add some color – that is all. The people talk into the night and the weeks that follow.

Five months later, the Matriarch reissues the invitation. It's identical to the first. She will supply the food and the entertainment. All each citizen need do is contribute a bottle of wine to the font. As the day approaches, excitement grows. When the Matriarch calls for their goblets to be filled, the people are silent.

The wine barely touches their lips before the people raise their voice in a cheer. The wine is splendid. More than the wine, though, their lives are splendid. In the months that followed the first gathering, neighbors continued the conversation and turned to each other, offering and receiving assistance. Those who stumbled were helped back to their feet. Thoughts of scarcity were gradually supplanted by acts of generosity.

It wasn't that the people were perfect, just as no pour of wine is perfect. And, of course, there were still a few who watered down their offering, but they were such a minority, it no longer impacted the quality of their life together.

They had decided who they would be. And the taste was superb.

―――

As if affixing a punctuation mark to end his story, the homeless man drains the remainder of his bottle, belches unceremoniously, and staggers off in search of facilities. Simon remains on the bench for some time before continuing his own journey. Watching people walk purposefully down the street, he wonders about their lives and contributions. Checking over his shoulder to confirm that his host isn't returning, he joins the others on the sidewalk.

He stretches his memory to draw links between the young girl in his office, the minister at the funeral home, and the man on the bench. They didn't look the same. They didn't sound the same. They certainly didn't act the same. And yet, the content of what they said held together.

Who were they and what did they want with him? And, if he did have a choice in the matter, should he tell them to bother someone else?

Simon opens his office door, half expecting the girl to be sitting in his chair. He hangs up his robe, but doesn't stop for the scotch. He's definitely had enough for the day. Without thinking, he checks that the hallway is clear before heading toward the exit.

It's not a long walk home, but Simon moves quickly, careful to avoid distraction, particularly of the human variety. He thinks about Ailish and what she might share at his funeral.

What would she say at his funeral?

Of course, wonderful things could be said about him, but weren't most of those simply part of his job? You can't exactly praise someone for visiting the sick when they're paid to visit the sick. And you can't expect marks for responding to calls in the middle of the night when 24-hour pastoral care is in your job description. And, again, you can't feel like you've gone out of your way to create a celebration for someone's life when there's an envelope of cash in your jacket pocket.

His pace slows. What could Ailish say?

It had been a while since they talked about anything substantial. Lots of chatting and organizing, but not much depth. That used to be his wife's domain, he tells himself.

But then he relents, perhaps it was his realm as well, but no longer.

A realization breaks into his thoughts. He's the old man pouring his plonk into the font. He's Barry without the sparkle.

As the idea takes hold, his unease grows. Standing in front of his house, Simon pulls out the envelope and mentally divides the money. Part will go toward bills: practical. Part will go to the drop-in shelter: contribution. He'll use the remainder to take Ailish out for breakfast and a dinner. That'll create some room to talk: relationship.

Arriving at the door, Simon takes a long, slow breath. He turns the handle.

CHAPTER FOUR

To an untrained eye, the elevator might seem a relic with its walls of stainless steel, empty phone box, and buttons that protrude black, plastic, and round – but those of us who use it regularly know that the way it conveys passengers between dimensions speaks more of Roddenberry than Dickens.

Here on the ground floor, I'm still connected to the main hospital complex, where patients are endlessly probed, drained, and/or scanned. Color-coded lines run along the walls, leading around corners through a maze of waiting and recovery rooms. These are the halls of the living and they reflect the frenetic energy of that relentless pursuit.

Yet with the push of a button, the doors of the lift close on this reality and open to another: a place set aside for the dying. There, the floor plan is simple, the pace unhurried, and the only interventions are those that ease pain. Not only is it the single remaining wing of the original hospital, it's a different world entirely from the rest.

As I make the transition in the elevator, I fall victim to a simple compulsion. Even though I know there's no phone in the box, I check every time, clicking the panel closed after verifying the constant nature of this place. The old lift stops abruptly, but accurately, at the third floor.

A serene volunteer offers me a cup of coffee, which I accept. It's good to be warm and occupied when the person you're visiting no longer responds. Years ago, I realized that I formulate some of my best sermons at bedside in hospice. There's a calmness about the place that lends itself to contemplation. I still go to the local bean shop for caffeine, but it gets noisy and expensive. Here, the coffee is free, the setting is quiet, and I handle two birds with one stone. Few things bolster a minister's reputation like spending a good chunk of time visiting the dying. Combine that PR with finding time to prepare a strong sermon and suddenly everyone's impressed.

Conveniently, Enid has been unconscious for the last few visits.

Walking the hall toward her room, I let the scent of coffee overwhelm other smells. My Scriptural text for Sunday already playing in my mind, I open the slightly ajar door without bothering to knock. Enid is lying under the covers with eyes closed, but sitting intimately on the end of her bed is another woman. Older even than my congregant, she smiles at me before returning her gaze to the unresponsive lids, "Enid, you have company."

Simon manages a smile for the woman and places his cup on the side table before taking Enid's left hand. It shows no sign of life other than warmth. Still standing, he turns to the other visitor, "I'm her minister, Simon. How do you know Enid?"

"Well, I've known her since she was a little girl." She looks to Enid, "Did you tell him how you climbed trees?" Then to Simon, "There was a huge cherry in her backyard. She would go right to the top, swaying with the wind, picking the ripest fruit. No child, boy or girl, dared to climb as high as her." Back to Enid, "And you knew it, didn't you, dear?"

Simon takes mental note of the story and the friend's affection, both great content for the upcoming eulogy. A few more revelations and it would write itself. Still holding Enid's hand, he allows his mind to set aside Sunday's message so that he can seize the unexpected opportunity, "What else can you tell me?"

A nod, "Enid had a pretty tough childhood. When she was barely more than a toddler, her older brother died. A grouse spooked his horse and he was thrown. Her parents couldn't redirect their sorrow and wouldn't get divorced, so it burned privately within the walls of their house. No one questioned why Enid wore long sleeve shirts on the hottest days of summer. She became an expert at keeping the bruises hidden."

Simon is dumbstruck. Not such a good story for his purposes and told with the same brevity and lilt used to describe the eating of cherries. "I never would have guessed a history of abuse. It seems Enid found a way through all of it. How did she manage to leave it behind?"

"Oh, I don't know if she ever left it behind, but she did put it in her garden."

This reference Simon understands. Having visited Enid in her semi-rural home, which she refused to leave until taken to hospice, he knew that the garden in the back was lovely, filled with flowering bushes and towering cedars.

At the time, he asked Enid about how she planned the layout and she confessed that no specific design existed. Each bush and perennial was individually placed in the name of a specific person – one with whom she struggled in the past or the present. Her practice was to hold the person in her thoughts each time she tended his or her plant. When she watered, when she weeded, when she built up the beds, it was a physical manifestation of her love for that individual. Rather than seeing it as a spiritual act, Simon thought it rather eccentric. Better than a house filled with cats, but not much.

Glancing now at Enid, he smiles at his jest.

As he does, Simon feels the presence of the friend, eyes on him. He hears the timbre of her voice shift, words taking on a familiar undertone, "What she did in the garden shaped what she was able to do beyond it. Remember the giant rhododendron in the Southeast corner? It was no more than a foot tall when she planted it for her parents. Now *some* might not appreciate the profound..."

His gut tightens. Had he made the cat comment out loud? No. Then why the shift? A shudder lying somewhere between outrage and dread peals through Simon's body. He makes the connection. Not again. Not here. Who are these people?

"...and the bed of dahlias. She planted those when her own son was driving her to distraction. By the time the buds were..."

Simon places Enid's hand back on her abdomen and faces the visitor, lowering his voice, "Okay, that's enough. You're with the others. What the hell are you doing here?"

"Whatever do you mean?"

"I suppose you have a story for me?"

"You're the one who asked."

"No, not her stories, the other ones."

"What are you talking about?"

"Who are you? You think I haven't noticed that you didn't give your name?"

Silently, the visitor stands so that she's across the bed from Simon. She claims Enid's right hand, holding it protectively between her own. Without pausing for punctuation, she volleys, "And who did you say you are? Strange bedside manner for clergy. Enid most certainly would not appreciate your tone."

Simon swallows.

She's simply a friend of Enid, nothing more. He searches for words but finds none, overwhelmed. What a mess. Stumbling over his own reaction, he mumbles something about a misunderstanding and flees the room, trying his best to do so at a dignified pace.

———

Stainless steel doors close. Ground floor button pushed, I focus on my breathing.

After her mother died, Ailish suffered from panic attacks at night. I found that if I asked her to track her breath, following it through her nostrils, all the way down into her expanding lungs, and then back up her trachea and out her mouth – she slowly regained control. When she didn't, I discovered that having her breathe into a small paper bag also did the trick, especially one that smelt of cookies.

I've no bag, but fortunately by the time the doors reopen, I'm calm. At least, I appear that way. It's the first time I've applied the technique to myself. I dab the remaining sweat from my brow with my shirtsleeve.

Still in the elevator, staring at the phone box, I contemplate an immediate return to hospice. How could I leave without offering a prayer for Enid? And what was I thinking when I confronted her friend? Enid needs a blessing and the friend deserves a proper apology.

But not now. I need to get my head on straight before I talk to anyone. I exit, passing hurriedly through the halls of the living and out the front doors. I start walking.

Before long, I realize that my head hurts – another casualty of my hasty departure from hospice. I step into Serious Coffee and get a cup to go. Once my body absorbs the caffeine, my headache should pass. Standing in line, it's clear that I'm still in flight mode, so I focus on the barista's craftwork. She prepares multiple orders simultaneously, but manages to offer individual attention to the final touches, shaping fir trees in the crème. I snap a lid over the fine art before departing.

I continue down the busy street, small shops lining both sides. Everyone on the sidewalk moves with purpose; it's the end of the business day for most. I give myself over to the flow, following the small social cues that prevent people from colliding without actually looking at anyone's face.

Several blocks further along, I'm getting out of breath and my pace slows, speed no longer necessary. At the same time, I'm not ready to rethink what happened in hospice.

Seeking distraction and a place to rest, I notice someone who stands out. Ahead, a young woman sits on a bench with her dog at her feet, a small shepherd cross. I get close enough to read her sign,

GREAT JOKES – TWO BUCKS

Though her hair suffers from dreads, the rest of her appearance is clean. Her eyes are a surreal green. I dig out a toonie, "Okay, I could use a good joke."

"You'll love this one." She stands up and her smile alone is worth the price. "Did you hear the sad news about Mickey and Minnie?"

I hadn't.

"Seems their marriage got so bad that Mickey took Minnie to court so that he could get a divorce. The judge, though, he couldn't see any grounds for breaking them up. He said, 'Look here, Mickey, you can't divorce Minnie just because she's a little silly.'" Dramatic pause. "And Mickey replied, 'You haven't been listening, judge. I didn't say that she's a little silly. I said that she's fucking Goofy!'"

The joke is terrible, but the delivery is disarmingly enthusiastic. I shake my head and offer a slight chuckle.

"Wow, tough crowd. Okay, you said you could use a joke, but maybe you need something more." She sits down again, stroking her dog, which drops its head onto her lap. Scratching between its ears, "Something longer. No swearing, I promise. How about a story?"

I find another toonie.

"You might as well get comfortable," she motions that I take a seat beside her.

In a time before time, there lived in the northern hills of India a massive Ox. It was of such size and strength that no other animal was its match. As he passed through the forest, even mighty Lion left him alone.

Yet despite his size and strength, Ox was known for his gentle nature – never exerting his power over other creatures. For this, he was treated with great respect.

One day, little Monkey decides to test this goodness. As the giant passes under his tree, Monkey drops a piece of ripe fruit on Ox's head. Landing with a thud, the fruit bursts, dripping down the great beast's forehead.

Ox stops only for a moment, looking neither to the right nor the left, neither up nor down. Then he continues on his way, unfazed.

Monkey remains undaunted in his mission. He drops another piece of fruit. Then another. Soon, Ox is dripping with juice from head to tail. Still, he looks neither to the right nor the left, neither up nor down. Instead, he alters his course and wades into a river, letting the current clean away Monkey's efforts, before chewing the lush grass on the opposite bank.

That evening, Monkey contemplates another test. He reasons that it's one thing to disregard fruit that might fall on its own accord. It's quite another to ignore a direct encounter.

The next day as Ox moves through the forest, Monkey slips down a vine and yanks the great beast's tail before scrambling back into the trees. Ox pauses for a moment. He looks neither to the right nor the left, neither up nor down, and continues on his way.

Monkey waits for an hour, then again slips down the vine and slaps Ox's behind before pulling his tail. Nothing.

At night, Monkey stares into the sky, plotting the next test. There must be some way to prod a negative reaction out of the giant.

The following morning, Monkey slides down his vine and runs alongside Ox, tickling his underbelly and poking at his flank. He climbs onto the magnificent animal's back and pulls at his ears.

Suddenly, in the midst of his revelry, Monkey realizes that Ox is no longer moving. The great beast displays no anger, not bothering to look to the right or the left, neither up nor down. He simply...waits.

Very slowly, Monkey reaches for a nearby vine and then quickly ascends into the canopy. Glad to be safe, he sets off to find dinner before plotting another test.

Keen eyes follow Monkey as he departs. They belong to Owl, who has watched the tests unfold and can no longer contain herself.

Having witnessed Ox's humiliation at Monkey's hand, Owl swoops down to offer the giant her support, "My great friend, you are the most powerful creature in the forest, even mighty Lion leaves you in peace. You could stop Monkey with a look, let alone a hoof. Why do you allow him to torment you?"

"My good friend, you are kind to be concerned, but you are mistaken. Monkey is not my enemy; he is my helper."

"Your helper? A minute ago, he was pulling on your ears."

"You know how I feel about my size and strength, how those qualities could define me. If I want to grow in character, I must embrace my opportunities as they arrive. When everyone treats you well, it is easy to be gentle; but to be gentle toward one who does not treat you well, that is a challenge. Monkey's assisting me in deepening my character."

"But Monkey thinks that he's in control."

"It does not matter what Monkey thinks, my dear Owl. It matters how I choose to respond."

―――

By the end of the story, the dog's head rests on Simon's lap. He slowly massages the soft ears as the young woman waits for his reaction. Pedestrians continue to rush along the sidewalk and cars jockey fiercely on the street, but to Simon, the world has slowed to its essence.

"I mistook a woman in hospice for one of you."

"That must have been awkward."

"Utterly."

After a while, Simon stops rubbing the ears. His hands barely leave their position before the dog puts an expectant paw on his knee. Obediently, Simon resumes the meditative task in silence as both he and the young woman watch the flow of people. The dog's eyes become slits; he's nearly asleep.

"Sometimes," she says, "I watch for hours. Everyone's so rushed, most of them preoccupied with their own worries."

"People have a lot of concerns."

"I think that people choose to have a lot of concerns. Many frame their life that way." She shifts position, "Then there are those like Enid, who have every reason to wear their hurt, but don't. They use it as fodder for reshaping their approach to the world." She stands, stretches, "Speaking of which, I think she's waiting for you. Don't worry, I'll take over with the dog."

———

I enter the elevator for a third time, feeling no compulsion to check the phone box. Stepping off, I accept the cup of coffee and make my way down the hall. Enid's door is slightly ajar, so I knock softly. No answer.

She's alone. I pull a chair up to her bed, sit, and take her hand in mine. Reaching over, I straighten a wayward strand of hair before apologizing for my behavior and abrupt exit. I tell her all that I remember about her garden, what I saw, the fresh scents, the sound of tiny birds flittering within the bushes. I'm surprised by what I can recall and suggest that, given my recent conduct, she might need to plant something in my name.

Enid smiles. Not a broad smile, but a definite raising of the corners. So unexpected. Delightful.

I spend an hour at her side, most of it in silence. When it comes time to leave, I offer a prayer and then bend over her bed to kiss her forehead. Close to her, I say, "Thank you."

The steel elevator doors close. I'm taken aback by the difference between this moment and the one only hours ago. Nothing external had changed. It has simply been reframed. I chuckle at myself. Not just silly. Fucking Goofy.

CHAPTER FIVE

When sermons write themselves, it's a testament to the divine spark. Thoughts fall into place. Examples ground concepts to concrete experience. Everything flows as if someone else's hands are at the keyboard. The minister as conduit, nothing more.

For me, it's an ecstatic experience that never happens at 7:00 on a Saturday night.

Tomorrow morning three hundred people will gather in the pews and every single one of them will watch me ascend into the pulpit. If I do well, what I offer in the next 15 to 20 minutes will be referenced during coffee hour and applied to real life. If I don't, comments will find their forum in the parking lot. Either way, the only direct feedback I'll receive will be pro forma compliments offered over a handshake as people leave the sanctuary.

Given the current blankness of the screen, I'll be lucky if they grab a coffee before heading outside to debrief. They think it's pretty straightforward. I've got a whole week to come up with something original. The problem is that they've already heard the passage a hundred times and balancing their diverse demands is a monolithic task. If I use too much humor, they'll call me glib. Not enough, and I'll be imperious. Too many references, and I'm ostentatious. Too few, I'm amateurish. Comparisons will be drawn to my predecessor, an extraordinarily gifted orator who happened to be a complete ass when not on display. Of course, their assessment will overlook the latter.

Hoping to ignite the divine spark, I pour a little more of my prized Ardbeg Uigeadails. Though most cut it with water because of the higher alcohol content, I prefer the sharpness of drinking it neat. Raising my glass, I allow the scotch to rest on my tongue before warming my throat. By slowing the process, I create room to savor the complex layers. I'm not sure whether I discern the "scrumptious fruit cake" noted on the box, but there's no denying the gorgeous smoke and peat.

Yet, despite the quality of the fuel, my screen remains blank.

When three hundred people spend 20 minutes listening to a sermon, it constitutes one hundred hours of time that no one gets back. If the uninspired sermon taints the whole service, it's roughly 375 hours lost. Equating the number to an individual's work life, that's ten weeks – more than two full months – down the drain. My economics professor would want me to also include the cost of lost opportunities, but the figures are already daunting.

My professional colleagues are at pains to downplay the relative significance of the sermon. In seminary, we're constantly reminded that the Eucharist stands at the center of the service, but even at that most polite moment of departure, no one shakes your hand and tells you that you were brilliant at tearing the loaf in two. When it comes to worship, clergy are measured by the quality of their time in the pulpit.

Feeling the inevitable approach of a headache, I replenish my glass so that I can avoid the onslaught with pre-emptive Tylenol.

Ailish enters the room, slightly out of breath from her run, one earbud dangling. The kitchen bears the usual markings of her father's Saturday nights. She watches him refill his glass and shakes her head. "You know, most people go drinking with their friends, not God."

The words are delivered with a slight smile, but there's an edge. Simon brushes aside his daughter's reproach. He's heard enough on the subject. "To each their own companion."

Ailish pulls a chair from the kitchen table and sits, "I imagine God has trouble keeping up with you."

"You forget the wedding in Cana?"

She reaches across the table and softly closes his laptop, "You know, Dad, back in the day, you didn't drink when you got stuck. You went for a walk."

"Back in the day, the walk worked because your Mom went with me. She was quite the muse."

Ailish steadies herself, gestures to the bottle, and pulls the trigger, "What do you think she'd make of her replacement?"

His response visceral, Simon yanks the plug from the back of the laptop and stands. He brings up his internal list, this being for him another reminder of why he can't wait until Ailish finds her own place. He drops a clamp on his temper but coldly declares, "Looks like I'll take that walk after all."

Six blocks later the fresh air cuts through the haze of scotch. Anger clears and pace slows. Simon remembers being connected to his daughter, witty banter their foundation block. Even that had twisted. Now most days follow a pattern of pleasant enough mornings followed by evenings marred by varying levels of tension. Initially, he put it down to Ailish going through a stage. Now he wonders whether it's time to resign himself to the ongoing reality. Before weighing the question, his pace again quickens as he remembers a more immediate challenge.

Ahead he sees a familiar sign where he can purchase several hours of late night productivity.

———

I regroup, boxing away her behavior until it can be addressed. I tell myself that it's hard not to settle into the right frame of mind for the sermon, ensconced at a familiar table in the back corner of the local Starbucks. Laptop open. Word engaged. Triple shot cappuccino about to be declared by an attentive barista.

Tapping in an initial thought, I hear my name called. I look to the counter, but no drink awaits. I must have misheard. Clearly, I need that shot of caffeine. Seconds later, my name again and still no cup. This time I notice that the voice isn't coming from behind the counter.

I follow the sound and see Louise, a long-time member of the congregation and a little old to be out at this time of night. I check for her grandson, who usually orchestrates her adventures, but she sits alone.

Smiling externally, I'm trapped. Unscheduled meetings in unofficial places are an inescapable part of the job. Suddenly missing the self-contained quiet of hospice, I make my way over to her table. As I pull out a chair, I look back at my laptop, lid closed, preserving the charge for a very late night.

"What are the chances of meeting you here tonight, Reverend?"

I know the answer. The chances are inversely related to the time I have available, especially as that number approaches zero. Before I find a more appropriate answer, she continues, "Well, you're exactly the person I need."

It's not easy to fake a smile. Inherently, humans are very perceptive about the wrinkles at the corner of our eyes. I do my best to mimic the slight squint, encouraging her to reveal what's on her mind.

Louise has a lot to share. The timeline is six months in length, marked by false positives, retesting, and a succession of specialists. Turns out that today she sat down with the senior oncologist to hear three realities. Because her cancer has spread, it's inoperable. Being stage four, it's imminently terminal. Originating in the pancreas, her passing will likely be painful.

"Not my best day."

I ready my list of condolences and assurances. "Louise, I'm so sorry..."

"No, that's not the direction we're going with this conversation. I've enjoyed 82 years of extraordinary health and I have a wealth of relationships to prove it. I've already won this game, even if it gets called tomorrow."

"That's a very brave approach."

"I wouldn't call it that. What choice do I have? I've got two months at the outside. It's how it is."

"It's still a choice. Not everyone would stay positive."

"What else am I going to do? I've got a few apologies to make and a lot of people to thank."

"You're worried about some of your decisions?"

"I've tried to live a good life, but it hasn't always worked out that way. You can be honest about that at my funeral. It's such a sham when people drone on as if the deceased were perfect. A bit of honesty works fine for me. Just make sure that you thank everyone for coming…and ask them why they didn't have anything better to do."

Her eyes testify a genuine smile. It's contagious.

"Now if you've got time, get your computer to take some notes, and I'll order you another coffee. Yours is cold on the counter. We have work to do."

Shortly after eleven, I usher Louise into a cab. Small wonder she left her oncologist baffled by her physical resilience in the face of the cancer's progression. Yet, knowing her, it makes sense. When we were still at the table, I asked what she thought was next for her after this life. She said that she didn't know whether she was going up or going down, but that if she was going down, it would be okay — she had a lot of good friends there.

———

"Quite a lady." The words echoing his own thoughts, Simon turns to find a twenty-something skater, complete with baggy clothes and longboard. Hair casting over his left eye, he leans against the lampstand, coffee in hand.

"That she is. Good night."

"Hold on. Don't you want to talk?"

"Afraid I don't have the time right now. Goodbye."

"Face facts, friend. It'll take four or five hours to get your sermon written and polished. By that time your sleep cycle will be so screwed it'll be too late to go to bed without waking up groggy. Better pull an all-nighter and sleep after church. If that's the path, you've got a couple of hours to kill."

Simon's sigh is audible. "Sounds like you have something you want to say." A little too tired to care, he decides to make the most of it, "Tell you what. Let's make a deal. I'll hear you out, but only if you tell me something about you and your associates."

"No problem, Monty."

Taken aback by the quick assent, Simon hesitates before nodding, "Go ahead, but get to the chase. I'm tired."

"Only a couple of questions." The skater takes a final draw from his coffee and moves away from the lamppost so that he stands closer to Simon. "What'dya notice about Louise's approach?"

"She's very positive, even courageous."

"Not asking for your judgement. We already gave her props. Go deeper. What'dya notice?"

"She talked like she didn't have a choice, but we both knew she did."

"Deeper. What did you notice about her choice?"

"She's absolutely clear about her commitment. I'm supposed to read Micah at her service, the bit about acting justly, loving mercy, and walking humbly with God. Louise says it captures everything she tries to do. She's also clear that there are days she doesn't live up to it. She's okay with that reality. No excuses. Very little guilt. Lots of learning."

"Sounds like she picked her approach, but what sets her apart from the crowd?"

Simon rolls through the possibilities before offering one, "She lives it when the stakes are high. Even with today's news, it's more than words."

"So how'd she get so good at it? Both we and Louise know there'll be days when she's going to struggle, but her act is clearly together. How'd she get so smooth?"

"I don't know. I didn't ask."

"Then I'll try to inspire some thoughts, but we better start walking you home." The skater separates the plastic lid from his paper cup and pops each into an appropriate bin. Kicking his board into place, he steps on and places a hand on Simon's shoulder. "You walk and I'll talk."

———

Long ago there lived a young woman who struggled with the decisions she faced. Her problem wasn't knowing what to do. She was often clear about what was right. The snag was in the doing of it.

Sometimes it was the approval or disappointment of peers or family that would sway her. Other times it was the lure of easier paths or immediate gains. It became such an ongoing struggle that she questioned whether something was wrong in the way she was formed.

Yet the youth knew that she wanted to live her life well, so she sought out the advice of her community's wisest Elder.

One night, the youth sees the old woman sitting alone at her fire. After standing a while at the edge of the light, the youth takes a seat across from the Elder and waits. Together, they watch the flames slowly diminish before settling into a glow of crackling embers encircled by round stones. The Elder reaches to her side and leans forward, placing a few more broken branches within the ring. Small flames lick at the fresh wood. "When you are ready, speak."

The young woman gathers her thoughts and begins to share. The Elder listens without comment, no sign of agreement or disagreement betrayed on her face. By the time the youth finishes describing the fight within herself, the fire is almost out.

The old woman reaches to her side and adds more branches. Once the flames cast their light, she clears her throat, "Since the beginning, there have been two wolves within us. The first wolf embodies all that is good — our capacity for generosity, for courage, for honesty. The second wolf represents all that is bad — our inclination towards jealousy, towards anger, towards selfishness. Not even the best of us lives free from the bad wolf. Not even the worst of us lives apart from the good wolf. They both live within us, but these creatures cannot live side-by-side in peace. They are locked in conflict until the day we depart this life."

The youth watches the flames dance over the Elder's face, whose eyes continue to focus on the fire, then asks, "Why is their fight so fierce within me?"

The old woman shifts the coals with a branch before throwing it on the fire. It quickly casts light more broadly around them. "The fight is no greater within one person than another. The difference lies in the person, not the wolves. Some of the most decent aren't aware of their wolves. Some of the least admirable are equally unaware. Your experience is different because you are very conscious of the wolves, nothing more."

The young woman begins to speak, but the Elder shakes her head, reaches to her side and hands over a branch.

The youth waits for the fire to burn down before adding the wood. Once it catches, she speaks, "If this is our reality, that both wolves are always present and that they will always fight, what can we do to live good lives?"

The old woman raises her head and grins, eyes reflecting the light of the fire, "Every day, we choose which wolf we feed."

Allowing this thought to fill her mind, the youth sits with the Elder. Neither adds branches to the fire. They share the last of the light until the embers fall silent.

Simon approaches his home, skater in tow. They, too, have fallen silent. The wheels of the board clack with the crossing of each sidewalk joint. The slight breeze is cooler and sweet, the day closer to dawn than dusk.

"You're my fifth. How many more should I expect?"

The skater releases Simon's shoulder and steps off his board. "Sorry, I can't give you a clear answer on that one."

"Come on, we made a deal."

"No need to throw shade, friend. I only said I can't offer a clear answer. If you're going to understand it, you need to drop that disposition towards assumptions we talked about and pick a new frame. It's time to let go and get intentional with your own story."

"Sounds like your group shares notes."

"Man, you're totally missing the point. What matters more, the messenger or the message? You're so focussed on the people doing the talking that you're hardly hearing what's being said. Give your head a shake. I'm telling you, it doesn't matter whether it's five people or a hundred."

"That's not much of an answer."

The skater frowns and puts his front foot on the board. "Next time, if you want a better response, think about your question. Don't rush. Wait for tea or fire or something. Take a page from the stories. Friend, sometimes it's like you're not listening to a word."

Pushing off with his back foot, he's down the sidewalk and onto the street. Simon turns towards the front door before the skater's out of sight.

Ailish left the hall light on. Usually, she flips switches and unplugs every electrical device on her evening Gore patrol. I'm thankful for the subtle gesture.

Walking down the hall past her room, I notice that her door is open. I look in.

The light casts across her sleeping face. Although she's an adult, I immediately reconnect to a thousand nights of checking on my girl before going to bed. I see myself putting away the storybook, straightening the sheets, and kissing her forehead. At the time I didn't fathom that a clock was ticking on these simple, childhood rituals.

Or that I would find myself in this state.

While replaying our argument through my head, I continue along the hall to the washroom, brush my teeth, and head to bed. I pull back the sheets and unbutton my shirt before I realize what I've forgotten and head back down the hall. Sitting down at the kitchen table, I replug my laptop and switch on the power. Reaching for the Ardbeg, I remember the wolves and set it aside for a more appropriate time, along with the skater's rant about messages and messengers.

With these thoughts safely boxed, I set my fingers to the keyboard and begin to fill the page. Morning will soon be here and I'm quickly running out of time.

CHAPTER SIX

Whereas good news can wait until morning, bad news has its own timeline. Dragged out of the ramblings of my subconscious, I note the clock as I pull the charger from my phone – 2:14 a.m. At least it's a Tuesday night, so no meetings first thing tomorrow. I mean, today.

"Hello? Yes, I know them. I'll be right over."

Decision time. I can throw on the last clothes I wore, jump in the car, and arrive as quickly as possible. Or, I can take a quick shower, put on fresh clothes, and arrive twenty minutes later, a little fresher, and more awake. Splitting the difference, I stick my head under the tap before brushing my teeth and grabbing a clean shirt.

I'm not comforted by the fact that the name spoken on the phone barely registers. Wracking my brain to make a more definite connection to a specific face, I come up empty. The sense of not knowing won't be out of place given the unpredictable nature of all things ICU. One more uncertainty won't make a difference.

After entering the hospital doors, Simon steps into a bathroom before taking the corridor that leads to the Intensive Care Unit. He checks himself in the mirror.

The delay isn't about style; it's about being prepared. Currently, he knows nothing of what lies ahead. It could be a stroke or a car accident or a knifing. The person he visits might be conscious or not, speared with tubes or not, quietly breathing or gasping for air. Hope might be expressed as the desire for full recovery or quick departure.

Whatever the individual's situation, it unfolds in the context of multiple patients lined up in side-by-side rooms, glass walls looking toward the central nursing station, where staff work to address everyone's needs in 12 hour shifts.

As a rule, each ICU patient is restricted to two bedside visitors for good reason. Guests can be exhausting, both for patients and for staff. It's not simply the numbers. It's the behavior. With so much on the line and so little that loved ones can do, it exposes people at their best and worst. All's fine when people rise to the occasion, but when someone doesn't, the visitor becomes a vortex, disrupting the energy and focus of patient and staff alike. Simon knows his role will center on the friends and family, allowing the hospital staff to concentrate on the patient.

With all this in mind, he no longer fusses with wardrobe. Leaving the washroom and turning the corner, his eyes are not on the entrance doors to the ICU, but on the waiting area adjacent.

"Father Simon!"

Absorbing the misapplied title and asking no questions, he lets the family follow their own pace and agenda. As everyone stands, the mother takes hold of Simon's hands and apologizes for having him summoned in the middle of the night. She recalls how he baptized their daughter, Bren, fifteen years ago and how appropriate it would be for him to offer prayers now.

Simon smiles and nods, but not because he's touched by the mother's desire for sacred rituals. Rather, he's amused by it, never quite grasping why people still want the formalities when they're not interested in sticking around for the rest of the package. It's like being really concerned about getting the right picture on a driver's license, while having no intention of getting behind the wheel of a car.

This being neither the time nor place to quibble over religious observance, he opts to offer comfort, "I'm glad you called."

Simon gestures for everyone to sit. Bren's parents take separate armchairs, holding hands across the divide, while her older brother and his girlfriend share the small couch. Simon sits on the identical couch opposite. Because the waits are often long and intense, the furniture outside of ICU is more comfortable than average. With surrounding plants, it feels like a living room set on a theater stage.

The father relates the practical details. Nothing more can be done. Up until twenty minutes ago, they'd been rotating their time at bedside. When everyone agreed that the situation was palliative, the staff asked them to wait outside while they disconnect the tubes to make Bren comfortable. He admits that it's probably more about making them comfortable, but that's okay. No need for all the paraphernalia. With the ventilator removed, it'll be a matter of a few hours.

Simon sits through the silence that follows. The girlfriend leans closer into the brother, wrapping her arm around his shoulders. Dad uses his free hand to rub his eyes. Starting with the mother, the family constructs their joint understanding of what happened.

They knew that Bren was under pressure. Pointed slurs at school found a wider audience through social media. Staccato outbursts marred what had been her dependably peaceful disposition. These she would consistently reel back, but it took conscious effort, as if you could see her deliberately wresting control from her amygdala.

Yet, she was a year into her transition and no one close to her doubted the decision to leave behind the vestiges of male identity. She had come so far, so decisively: meeting with her school's counselor and administration, building gender awareness among her peers, researching what degree of reassignment might meet her needs. Along with Amnesty. Along with Soccer. Along with AP's.

Most importantly, after years of living on the edges of different circles, she found friends who were an amazing, eclectic group of supportive minds. She referred to them as her tribe. In so many ways, she seemed set.

This morning, Bren made a sandwich and headed for school, while her parents went to work. Before her coffee break, the mother received an automated call saying that Bren hadn't shown. With no response from Bren's cell or the home line, she returned home to investigate.

There she found Bren unconscious, an empty bottle of pills at her side, along with a note that was both an apology and an expression of gratitude. It contained no censure, no explanation. By the time she arrived at ICU, it was too late. When they decided to withdraw life support, Simon was called, bringing them to this moment.

The ICU door opens and a nurse steps out. At first, only the mother stands to go in with Simon, but he glances at the nurse, who nods. He gestures that the others rise, "Let's go together."

The rule no longer applies.

The slight breeze feels good after so many hours in a room without windows. I leave my car in the lot, avoiding the enclosed space. Having watched Bren's last breath, the part of me that still feels it's night could use a drink. The part that realizes it's early morning wants to find a coffee. A third part searches the horizon for one of the storytellers. I have words I'd like to share.

Hard to put a finger on what I'm feeling, something within the constellation of frustration, sorrow, and anger.

As I walk down the street, I keep an eye out for past faces and likely suspects. I know they'll come to me, but this time I want to be the one doing the finding. I've got questions for the sagacious bastards. In fact, it would be great to get them all at the same table, no more games.

After an hour of quick walking, I drop into a Mocha House and order a cappuccino, dry-to-stay. Minutes later, I'm sitting at one of the street tables, waiting for someone to join me. I check my watch, irritated, as if my counterpart were late for a tightly scheduled appointment. Drinking quickly and not bothering with the last of the foam, I return to the counter for a second cup. By the time I'm back outside, the seat across from mine is occupied.

"Rather impatient, aren't you?" Cracking open a can of Coke, the sizeable man wears military fatigues. Given the grey in his beard and lack of hair on his head, he must be close to retirement.

Not fond of uniforms, my already agitated state worsens. I counter a little too sarcastically, "It's just that I can't wait to hear the next story."

The uniform doesn't pick up the gauntlet. He simply frowns, "Disappointing."

"Disappointing?"

"You're in the room when she dies. You witness the anguish of her family. You feel you've got questions that need answering. And yet you wrap your energy around what I'm wearing and how long it took for me to show up." He leans forward, "I'm calling bullshit. Start over."

I gather my thoughts, "Why did Bren need to die?"

"Everyone dies. After all that bluster, I thought you'd articulate a more substantive question."

"Yes, everyone dies, but why her?"

"Why not her? You might as well ask why some babies die at birth while others live into their nineties. There's nothing unnatural about it. Happens all the time, all over the world. Get to the real question."

"Okay, then who's responsible for her death?"

"Seriously? That's all you've got?" Takes a swig from his can, "Fine. You first, Simon. You've been stomping around for hours, you must have some thoughts."

"Her family seems solid. She was well supported. I'm thinking that the bullying got out of hand. It's one thing to face it at school, but once it hits social media, it becomes omnipresent. I'm guessing she got overwhelmed."

"So you're placing the blame at the feet of the bullies and the bystanders?"

"Well I'm sure as hell not going to place it at Bren's feet."

"Why's that? She's the one who downed the pills."

"Oh, so you prefer to blame the victim." My voice is louder than intended. People from other tables turn their heads towards us, then instinctively look the other way.

"Small wonder you have trouble coming up with a good question. You have trouble telling the difference between a query and a statement. Simon, slow down. I'm not putting this at any particular person's feet."

"Then what do you think's behind her suicide?"

Another swig, "Now that's a better question." The uniform reaches into his pocket for a regulation kerchief and wipes his beard, "For me, it all comes down to our dance with fear."

Although he pauses as if the statement says it all, I know what comes next.

Once in a kingdom long ago, there lived a powerful Sultan. Although wiser and kinder than most of his contemporaries, the Sultan had enemies who sought his death. Because of this, he began to search for a personal physician, not only to look after him in times of illness, but to heal him should his enemies strike.

Physicians from across the lands made their way to the Sultan's capital. Some were drawn by the prestigious and profitable nature of the position. Others sought to preserve and extend the reign of a ruler they perceived to be just. After many interviews and tests, the long list dwindled until only two candidates remained. Both were exceedingly competent at their craft.

One day, the Sultan calls them to his court, "Of all who stepped forward, only you two remain. Given that medicine is your specialty, not mine, tell me how I should decide between you?"

Both men are silent, pondering the question, until one, much taller than the other, speaks first, "Your excellency, the greatest danger to people in your position is poisoning. I propose that you lock my colleague and me into a wing of your palace, along with the tools of our art. The one who knows best how to poison and how to heal himself will be your physician. Your choice will be obvious, because after the test, there will only be one of us left."

"I bow to your experience," responds the Sultan, "providing that your colleague agrees."

The shorter physician takes a moment before answering. To his mind, taking the life of another to promote one's own interests was anathema to his oath as a physician. Yet even though the proposition goes against his values, he does not want such a man as his colleague to become the Sultan's physician, so he consents, "I accept this challenge, but I have vowed to protect life, never to take it. Because of this I will protect myself, but I will not attack my colleague."

The men are escorted to their rooms, locked away from the rest of the house and the world outside.

That night, before drifting off to sleep, the shorter physician notices that a powder has been spread on his pillow. Rising immediately, he gathers his equipment and identifies which antidote he must prepare.

The next morning, a bowl of fruit sits on the breakfast table. Both men eye each other suspiciously. The taller demands that the shorter choose a piece of fruit, which he does. The taller then asks for his colleague to relinquish the fruit. Without argument, the shorter physician hands over the apple. After taking a bite, the taller stammers, "You tricked me. You chose the fruit you poisoned, knowing that I'd take it from you. Your pious words were lies!" Apple in hand, he runs back to his room to mix an antidote.

Throughout the week, the shorter physician discovers poisons on things he might eat or touch. His colleague is clearly well traveled, using plants, venoms, and minerals from the edges of the known world.

As the contest continues, the taller of the two begins to perceive every catch of dust as a threat. "You are waiting, thinking that I'll let my *guard down, but I haven't. Here, I've discovered your poison again!"* With such words, he runs to prepare another antidote, each one more perilous than the last. Soon, the taller physician refuses to eat or drink at all. He doesn't sleep lest there be an attack at night. Finally, not wanting to touch the handle of his door, he sits on the ground, unable to exit his room.

The next day, the shorter of the two finds him, tightly curled on the floor, dead.

After the doors are opened to the rest of the palace, the remaining physician stands before the Sultan, "I am sorry to report that my colleague did not survive."

"Congratulations, the position is yours," the Sultan continues, "but tell me, what became of your oath?"

"I kept my vow, but sadly, my colleague did not believe me. He consumed many antidotes that he didn't require and denied himself nourishment and sleep."

"So he wasn't poisoned?"

"In truth, my Sultan, he was taken by the most powerful poison of all – his own fear."

The uniform drains his Coke and places it beside Simon's cup and saucer. Traffic on the sidewalk and street reaches its morning peak. The workday has begun. Simon's own pace has slowed somewhat, the story having shifted his energy.

It doesn't blunt his desire for answers, "You've been using my name. If we're going to have a conversation, perhaps I can know yours."

"Does it matter?"

Simon quips, "Only if you don't mind me choosing one for you."

A wry smile flickers across the uniform's face, "In that case, let's keep it simple. Call me Death."

Simon shakes his head and sniggers, "Code name or gamer handle?"

He shrugs, "You asked. I answered."

"Yah, I'm not going to call you that."

"Then let's move on."

Picking through his thoughts, Simon searches for a summary statement, "So, you're saying that fear is bad."

"No, fear is essential. It's what keeps us alert to the possibility of danger. When we lived in caves, it kept us from taking unnecessary risks; it prepared us to enter the fray or froze us in our tracks. Our hard-wired response to fear saved us from taking too much time to think. Without it, we wouldn't have survived."

"Then why the story?"

"Fear has its place, but unless you're on the battlefield or about to be mugged, it's seldom helpful. These days we attach fear to things that don't represent actual danger. We're afraid that our boss will be upset or that our partner will leave us or that our friends won't approve. With any of these things, there's nothing to fear at a survival level, but we push the chemical panic button."

Simon nods. He knows this material, "And when we push that button, we don't think clearly. We only react."

"Exactly. There's a space for reflective thought between any event and our reaction. When we let fear hold sway, we bypass the space, and relinquish control to our base instincts. The taller physician enters the challenge imagining that he's in control, but once his fear takes center stage, he doesn't need enemies to destroy him."

"What about Bren?"

"You're the cleric. What do you think?"

"The bullies had no reason to attack her, other than the need to feel dominant and preserve their own status. They acted on that fear impulse, even though Bren posed no threat. Cruel."

"Perhaps, and at the same time all-too-human, primordial."

"And Bren, maybe she bought into it. Let it get under her skin. Stupid."

The uniform's sigh is audible, "Enough, already." He rubs his temple before gathering steam, "Must you always latch judgement onto your thoughts? 'Those people are cruel. This person is stupid.' Honestly, you exhaust me. And so fucking arrogant. That 'stupid' girl conquered more fears in her short span than most people notice in their lifetime. Kids her age lose sleep over a pimple. She was openly addressing contradictions in her core identity while on public display."

"Look, I didn't mean to…"

"You're in no place to judge how others face their fears, Simon. Hell, look in a mirror. You can't even deliver a sermon without fretting over what people might think of you, let alone face up to what's become of your relationship with your daughter. You'd rather avoid the unpleasantness of anything that might mess with your image. You want to criticize Bren? At least she took on her challenges. You should be striving to figure out how you can take a page from her book. You're so fearful of letting go and figuring out your place in this world that your identity is growing as shallow as the façade you tack on in the morning."

"Hey!" Simon protests. "There's no need to get personal."

"Actually, you do need to get personal." The uniform taps the table with his index finger. His tone shifts, slows. "You need to decide whether this is all you want out of life. It's up to you, but if you do want something more, you've got to start writing a different story." He stands and picks up the can from the table before leaving one last thought, "Simon, you're running out of time."

Without comment, he watches the uniform walk out of sight. It takes that long for the comment to sink into place. Simon checks his watch. It's still not 9:00. The whole day lies before him and he's exhausted by the prospect.

CHAPTER SEVEN

Sitting in my underwear, legs dangling over the side of the examination table, I'm transported back to age twelve. As I shift slightly to better read the anti-smoking and birth control posters pinned to the walls, the white paper beneath me crinkles. I hear my chart slide from its holder before the double knock and entry.

Stethoscope slung around her neck, the doctor and I exchange pleasantries, including my apology for being a bad patient. The hours and location of the local clinic proved too tempting in recent years, but I'm back. During my confession, she holds the stethoscope's diaphragm against her palm so that it's warm by the time she presses it to my chest.

"So, Simon, why the sudden desire for a physical?"

Fortunately, the taking of deep breaths provides time to find an answer. What I can't tell her is that an enigmatic collective of strangers has been offering bits of wisdom attached to dead or dying people, and that the last one warned I'm personally running out of time.

I'm looking for a heart and prostate check, not a psych assessment.

Between intakes I tell her it's past due that I should take better care of myself. She agrees, sending me on my tapped and prodded way twenty minutes later, blood work requisition in hand. Unless the results suggest otherwise, I appear to be in sound health.

Though I reassure myself that this is good news, the verdict offers little comfort. Once outside, I check my messages. Apparently, I was missed.

A symbiotic relationship exists between clergy and funeral homes. Because people often want a minister to preside at their loved one's service, but don't necessarily want a traditional liturgy, the parlors are constantly searching for ministers who are flexible in their approach. At the same time, clergy, many of whom are chronically underpaid, find themselves keen to make an extra dollar while still exercising their calling.

Which explains the message left for Simon, but not its content.

As usual, he received a name, an age, a cause of death, and a contact person. Oddly, this was followed by the name of a restaurant and a request to join a 7:00 reservation, no need to call unless the time doesn't work.

Simon puzzles over the invitation. It's not that it shouldn't happen this way. It simply didn't. One might gather in a living room, an office, or even a coffee shop, but never in all his years had Simon been invited to dinner in a situation where he wasn't well acquainted with those involved.

Which goes some way to explain his unease on this cloud-covered evening as he stands in front of the venue, contemplating the posted menu. Its pricing doesn't seem to deter the flow of young, fashionable souls who saunter past. With each swing of the door, lively music assaults his drums, more like a bar than a restaurant. Not exactly the place to plan a funeral.

It now being a little past 7:00 and not wanting to appear rude, Simon takes the plunge. The place is packed with various sized groups sitting around constellations of small tables and along a bar. Upon hearing his name, the waiter leads Simon through the crowd, around a corner and down a mirrored hall. Much to Simon's relief, he finds himself in a quieter setting. An elaborate anime mural adorns the wall to the left, while to the right stands a floor-to-ceiling collection of wines and spirits. Massive windows expose the street front.

The waiter pulls out a seat, placing Simon across from a sharply attired man in his early seventies.

"Thank you for agreeing to meet me here. I suspect it's unusual."

I smile, appreciating the acknowledgement. We exchange pleasantries and I offer my condolences. Not wanting to be in the meeting all evening, I pick up my menu.

"One more indulgence, if I may," he continues. "Arjun was the love of my life and you didn't know him at all. My hope is that by the time you leave, you'll get a glimpse of the man. And if you'll allow me, you might start with the food he savored. Because of his heart, he had to behave, so any time the rules were broken he made sure it was worthwhile. Might I order for you?"

Most unusual, indeed, but I soon discover that I'm in good hands. Clearly, this couple knew their way around a menu. Moments later, I'm sipping a gin that's been muddled with mint and ginger. Soon afterwards, our waiter places before me steamed clams with lemongrass and sausage, followed by Javanese salmon with spiced sweet soy sauce, spinach, and fried leeks. Not simply good food, Arjun's favorite meal is breathtaking in its presentation, texture, scent, taste, and balance.

Through it all, I find myself scribbling notes. Arjun was 82, a decade older than his partner of forty years, an eccentric schoolteacher, an avid photographer, an entertaining and devoted friend, but most of all, an investor.

"But don't get me wrong," my host leans forward for overt emphasis, "I'm not talking money. Arjun invested in people – himself and others."

Between bites, my host offers a banquet of detailed examples.

As a teacher Arjun opened himself to the latest pedagogical developments, testing them in the classroom and noting how well his students learned before finally adapting them into his ongoing practice. He neither followed nor defied the crowd. Rather, he took the best of what it offered. This was his way, whether the subject be teaching, photography, or food. Arjun informed himself on the trends, separated the fad from the useful, and invested, becoming a more nuanced teacher, photographer, and foodie. He revelled in the growth, right to the end.

Even the recently discovered restaurant reflected this quest. Already a fan of Asian fusion, he became intrigued by the Deejay Café model, which led him to this place. That most of the clientele were in their thirties only sweetened the deal, ensuring that his ears would be stimulated along with his pallet.

On cue, our waiter arrives with dessert, a chocolate torte with spicy ice cream and peanut ganache. Unexpected and sublime.

Not a fan of his mandatory retirement, Arjun continued teaching as a tutor, investing in students whose needs were as much emotional as academic. He'd receive calls from school counselors and principals, requesting that he make room on his roster for one more. Over time, those who sought help with chemistry and math left with a better understanding of their identity and life options. Arjun became their significant, committed, non-related adult. A touchstone in the midst of their chaos.

He also nurtured a small, but vastly diverse group of friends, joking that he could never invite them all to the same party because there'd be blood on the floor. Even with these, he shared very little of himself, knowing far more about them than they knew of him. When pressed by his partner about this disproportional reality, Arjun said that he wasn't sure whether it had something to do with control, with insecurity, or both. Invariably, he'd then point out that he was a work in progress, "Add it to the list."

After decaf Americanos and more conversation, the bill arrives, thankfully straight into the outstretched hand of my host. He elects to stay for another coffee, but understands that I should go. As I make my way down the mirrored hall and into the cacophony, I imagine the first time an octogenarian Arjun stepped into this hive – the expression on his face.

The rain steady, Simon scans the street for temporary shelter. Hunching his shoulders and dropping his head, he hurries toward a bus stop at the end of the block, where he signals a cab that immediately pulls to the curb. Simon congratulates himself on his luck until a red haired woman in her fifties cuts in front of him, opens the rear door and takes the seat behind the driver. She pats the seat beside her, "No use standing out in the rain. Who knows how long it'll be."

Simon, about to decline the offer, stops himself. There's a shift, an almost audible click, as if a door opened within himself, offering space to consider his options. He bends over, sticks his head into the cab. Nothing to fear. The rain falls on his back, but only for a moment. Simon overrules his initial impulse and takes a seat.

He says, "Kind of you to offer me a seat in my cab. Where are we going?"

Twenty minutes later, they're sipping coffee in an oversized bookstore, the scent of caffeine enhanced by the musty fragrance of old volumes. Though some are chatting, most of the other patrons are sitting quietly with their purchases.

As she holds her cup with both hands and drinks, Simon notices a drop of water collect on her cheek before falling from her face. He surprises himself with how much at ease he feels. It's more than the repetition of the gatherings. There's something deeply familiar about this particular encounter.

Simon opens, "You take me to a book store to tell me a story? I feel like a kid."

"Describe the feeling."

"Some anticipation, excitement. A bit like anything might happen."

She turns at angle to the table, one leg crossed over the other, comfortable, "Not a bad state of mind."

"Could be the gin or the meal or you. Life's possibilities seem very open at the moment."

"Good to hear. And it's not a bad segue for our story."

There once was a man about to depart on a long journey. As part of his preparations, he calls upon three servants to tend his property. He distributes eight talents between them, a massive sum equivalent to over 150 years of a laborer's wages. Each receives according to his ability. To the first, he entrusts five talents; to the second, two talents; and to the third, one talent.

Having made safe his fortune, the man leaves.

Not knowing when his master might return, the first servant immediately takes his talents and starts trading with them, eventually making five more talents. The second does likewise, also doubling his master's money. The same is not true for the third servant, who finds a quiet place to safely bury his one talent.

After a long time, the master of these servants returns and calls upon them to settle their accounts. They gather with others in his great hall.

When the first servant steps forward, he says, "Master, you entrusted me with five talents. By trading with those, I made five more."

The master praises the servant, "Well done, good and faithful servant. You acted well with a little, so you will be given much more. Enter into the joy of your master."

Next, the second servant rises and says, "Master, when you left, you handed me two talents. Those I took and traded, making two more."

As with the first, the master praises his second servant, "Well done, good and faithful servant. You acted well with a little, so you will be given much more. Enter into the joy of your master."

Finally, the third servant stands to settle his account, "Master, you are a hard man, reaping where you don't sow and gathering where you don't scatter. Knowing this and being afraid, I hid the talent you gave me in the ground."

With overstated calm, the master delivers his response, "You wicked and slothful servant. So you know that I reap where I don't sow and gather where I don't scatter? Then at the very least you ought to have invested my money with the bankers so that I'd receive my own plus interest."

The master turns to the others, raises his voice, "Take his talent and give it to the one who has ten. For to everyone who has, more will be given, and there will be abundance. But from the one who has not, even that will be taken away. Cast this worthless servant into the outer darkness, where there will be weeping and gnashing of teeth!"

———

"Worst story ever," Simon shakes his head. "I wondered when your lot would get around to telling a story from my tradition and when you finally do, it's not one of our best."

Rather than entering the argument, his cab partner avoids the gauntlet, "Tell me about it."

Simon takes a breath, "Well, for starters, the story itself isn't very clear. Scholars argue over the translation and whether the master 'entrusted' the talents to the servants or 'gifted' them. Also, there's no indication as to whether or not the third servant is justified in his negative perception of the master. Even the comment about bankers and interest causes confusion because some commentators read it as sarcasm while others interpret it as greed."

"And?" she extends.

"And regardless, the whole thing is unfair and disproportionate. The master already has an idea of who's more capable given that the talents were awarded according to ability. Next, there's no indication that the servants receive any instruction about his expectations for the talents. So, already destined for failure, the last guy gets hammered with an overwhelming punishment, which, by the way, totally breaks any realism in the narrative flow. I appreciate that parables are supposed to have surprise endings, but this one pushes the credibility of hyperbole. It's one thing to catch the audience's attention and quite another to blow up the stage."

"So?"

"So what we get is a hugely manipulated story that's embedded in our collective psyche and used to rationalize financial privilege, because our divine being rewards the making of money with the making of even more money. At the same time, we're not obliged to worry about the poor because they've obviously been unwise and slothful in their life choices and deserve not only their poverty, but further impoverishment."

"Want to take a swing at other interpretations?"

"Sure. Wonderfully trite pieces about how we need to use our non-financial talents, which again allow the superior to feel superior, while the inferior underachieve as a consequence of their own moral failing. Either that, or gritty interpretations from some liberation theologians about how we need to stand with the third servant as he serves truth to the master, without fearing punishment. The story is a theological and intellectual black hole."

Enjoying his fervor, she teases, "Finished your tantrum?"

Somewhat embarrassed for getting worked up, Simon takes a breath and offers glibly, "If you want, I could go on."

"For what it's worth," she overrides, "I didn't tell the story for the sake of exegetical analysis. For our purposes, I'm not concerned about its original intent. Neither am I expecting any single story to offer a nuanced worldview. That's why we have more than one." She pauses as if waiting for Simon to catch up to her train of thought, "Sometimes stories are at their best when we simply allow ourselves to be mindful of the thoughts they elicit, and the great stories are worth repeating because they hit us in different places and levels at different points in our lives. It's not about the story having one for-now-and-for-all-time meaning. It's about the interaction between story and listener. The value of any story lies not in itself, but in the degree to which we're impacted." She shifts in her seat, takes a sip, "Following?"

Simon is more than following. Getting caught in the rain. Finding the bookstore. Sitting over coffee. The humor. The jostling of ideas. His rants. Her balance. Suddenly, he makes the connection. All of this is reminiscent of any half decent day with his wife – he'd almost lost memory of the sensation she provoked. He knows it isn't her seated across from him, but their exchange taps into something previously lost.

Enthralled in the moment, Simon delivers their old retort, "Lay on, Macduff."

She pauses, as if deciding whether to be side-tracked by the phrase. Instead, she brings him back into the conversation by building on her previous thought, "So, let go of your baggage, think about your day and retell the story to yourself. What do you notice?"

Simon is back in the doctor's office, white paper crinkling under him, worrying about his mortality. Next he finds his way to the Javanese salmon and Arjun, definitely someone who made the most of every good thing life affords. Then, to this moment, this feeling, this way of being present. He had as much as buried it with his wife. Of course, he should have done more with it, but at the time he was so sad, so afraid of further loss. And yet, to bury such a gift? Simon feels deserving of his own hyperbolic reprimand, but doesn't want to disturb this particularly content moment.

Instead of answering, he asks, "What's your name?"

"I thought we were focusing on the message."

She uncrosses her legs, straightens herself, and puts her elbows on the table. Hands clasped with thumbs supporting her chin, she looks across to Simon, "So, Macbeth, back to the story. What did you notice?"

If ever there was a night for a solo walk in the rain, this was it. Head swirling, I strike out in the direction of home, hoping to stumble across some tidy mental box by which to comprehend and compartmentalize, some way to label and file all of it.

Instead, tears. They fall freely down my face, diluted by the rain. They start as soon as I step alone onto the street. My thoughts flow, following one another like movements in a symphony, connected but distinct.

At first the tears are for my wife and all she missed, especially the last five years with Ailish. I keep walking, head down, pushing through the weather. At some point the tears attach themselves to my own loss, all the hopes and plans left unfulfilled because she's gone. The rain stays constant and I pick up my pace. Another movement opens and the tears are tied to the losses I imposed on myself. So much buried in the ground. So much squandered to ease my fear, that self-administered poison. Then, forty minutes into the soggy journey, the tears themselves subtly shift, joined now to the sensation I experienced in the bookstore. Rediscovery. As if so much of what was wrongly buried were back in my hand.

No boxes neatly labeled. Something better. I raise my face to the rain and let it do its work.

CHAPTER EIGHT

"So what madness does this day entail?" Ailish divvies out the granola into small ceramic bowls. Non-matching mugs steam with coffee. Part of the ritual, both drink their first cup black.

Setting aside the obvious, Simon picks something explicable.

"I don't know if it qualifies, but I've been asked to partake in a picnic lunch with an elderly lady from the church. She's a fairly new member, but apparently she does this every year to mark her wedding anniversary. Husband died eight years ago."

She chuckles, food in her mouth, then swallows, "Whether it qualifies as madness depends on your duties as stand-in spouse."

"Well, that's thought provoking!"

Not at all what she expects, Ailish scolds, "Dad!"

"Your mom has been gone for a while…"

Hands now on ears, "Too far! Too far!"

Simon gestures that she put down her arms, and switches tone. He's ready.

"I don't think I've told you how much our mornings mean to me. Not just your mom's granola, but this block of time we spend together. I know that things haven't been easy and I've not exactly been talkative."

"Mornings are good for me, too," she takes a breath, "but I've got to say, our evenings suck."

"You're right and most of it lies with me."

"Not looking to blame…"

"I know, but like I said, I've been the one holding back since your mom died. So what do you say we switch stations — more talk/less rot. Starting tonight. Deal?"

"Wow. If we can discuss your 80's humor, sure." Then, with her smile and a hint of diffidence, "You really like the granola?"

Parking the car at the base of the hill, I head up the path towards the outlook. Even in the midst of the city, it's a quiet spot, overlooking the water and piers to the mountains beyond. The day is perfect. Not a cloud in the sky and a cool breeze to keep the temperature within reason.

I'm not sure what to expect. No two people deal with loss in the same way, and there is no right way. I've known widows and widowers who pull the drapes and cut themselves off from the world on their anniversaries. Others make a point of meeting with family or friends. I let my own pass without a word.

Now walking along the viewpoint, I see her waving in the distance. She's on a bench nestled under the speckled shade of an oak tree. Shaking hands, I notice a wicker picnic basket at her feet. When I join her, she places it between us and opens the lid. Soon cucumber sandwiches and chocolate chip cookies find their way onto small china plates. Freshly squeezed grapefruit juice pours into tumblers.

"I want you to know that I'm not always this selfish," she confesses. "For all the other days – his birthday, the day he died, Christmas, those sorts of days – I let family and friends look after me. But today is our anniversary so I do something just for me." She bites into a cookie, chews, swallows, the silence natural. "I take someone to this bench, Mateo's favorite." She gestures, pointing out one of the piers in the distance. "See, we spread his ashes in the water down there so that it's part of the view." She touches my shoulder, bringing me back to the immediate moment. "On our anniversary, I take someone to this bench and tell them one story about Mateo. Yes, don't worry. Only one." Her smile is incredibly charming. "This doesn't work with family and friends, because they already know the stories. So, I bring someone new into his circle. Can you forgive this selfishness?"

I want to suggest that it's not a selfish act, but then realize it's not a point to be won. "Of course."

She pats my knee twice with her hand, "Then you keep eating and I'll start talking."

When Mateo was in his late thirties, their eleven-year-old daughter was struck by a drunk driver. At the time, only the regional facility offered the kind of rehabilitative therapy necessary for such a complex spinal injury. While his wife looked after the rest of the family at home, Mateo closed the doors on his practice to be at his daughter's side.

This entailed visiting her daily for an entire year in her four-person, co-ed unit. She was always the youngest, her roommates ranging in age from their teens to their thirties. The spinal injuries were varied, but all were severe, making the basics of life challenging.

The orderlies and nurses were always pressed for time. This meant that everything less significant than the injuries themselves took second place. Simple pleasures like washing one's face or brushing one's teeth weren't necessarily going to happen, let alone the timely delivery of a cup of water or extra blanket. Even when food services placed a meal on the table beside the bed, some patients couldn't swing it into place. For those in traction, window blinds administered slow torture as the beam of sunlight slowly crossed the room until it shone directly in their eyes; even the sun mundanely moving through the sky created a need for assistance.

Which is what Mateo did for his daughter. Day after day, he washed her face and brushed her hair. When the food came, he placed a towel to catch the drips, cut the food into bite-sized pieces, and helped her get the fork to her mouth. The feeding was especially challenging during the weeks she spent in a Stryker frame. It basically allowed her to be sandwiched in complete spinal traction, rotating her from back to front every four hours. If she happened to be facing down at mealtime, Mateo sat on the floor and fed her from below. Each of these activities was further complicated by the presence of constant pain, along with the side effects of the drugs used to mitigate its intensity.

"But that's not the point of the story," she says, interrupting her narrative. "Most wonderful of all was that once Mateo finished whichever task with our daughter, he turned his attention to the others. Often they didn't have their own families in town, so he cut their meat, wiped their chins, and closed the blinds when the sun hit their eyes."

She pauses. I nod as I swallow, readying a compliment, but she's not finished.

"And when you think about it," she continues, "at times this meant serving people who were at fault for their predicament, including some who drove drunk." She checks whether I understand the implication, tapping my knee, "Do you see? Some of those patients could just as well have been the person who broke our daughter's back." She recoils from the thought. "It was a staggering realization, especially for me. Yet there he was, recognizing their pain, soothing their anxiety." She smiles, "And not out of some distorted sense of obligation. He went around the room simply because he was that type of guy, regardless of the weather."

She sighs happily, shakes her head, "Honestly, if he did anything other than help, he'd have lost a piece of himself." Another tap to my knee, like a child sharing a treasured secret, "It's one of the things I really loved. He didn't let outside things change him."

Taking another cookie, she falls silent. We enjoy the view and the breeze. Though I ask for more, she sticks to her promise of one story. "After all," she says, "today is about me."

After a final wave, Simon leaves behind his car and strides fifteen minutes down the hill back into the crowds until he finds himself at the waterfront, walking along the pier that seems closest to the spot where Mateo's ashes were spread.

Tourists and locals walk the wooden slats of the long wharf. Some stop and sit on the benches made from stacked blocks of large dimension wood at the center. Others lean against the outer railings, careful to avoid the evidence of birds.

Simon leans against the rail, eyes to the distance.

"You look like someone who needs a fishing line," offers the man to his left. Simon takes a few steps in his direction and looks in the white bucket at his feet. Usually, Simon does his best to not engage in these sorts of conversations, but he feels drawn.

"Looks like you've had a good day," Simon notes. The man's weather worn face grins, a sun bleached Tilley hat perched on his head.

"It's not the number of fish in the bucket that makes it good. It's the fishing."

Catching the subtle depth of the statement, Simon wonders how these people know where he's going before he does, and then quickly discards the thought. Best to focus on the message.

"And what appeals about fishing?"

The man adjusts his hat and then his line, "I guess it's the pace, for one. Everything slows down and comes into focus. We need moments like this to get our heads clear. I remember how I used to come down after a bad day at work or an argument with my wife and it didn't take all that long for things to kind of fall into place. I could see my strengths and shortcomings more clearly, which led to better thinking. Well, until the next time I stepped in it." He laughs and Simon joins. This guy, he likes.

"Last month," Simon keeps the ball rolling, "I went to a seminar and the speaker talked about how we need to focus on our strengths because we're never going to get far chasing our shortcomings."

"Oh sure, our strengths should be the focus," the fisher agrees, "but we should never lose sight of our shortcomings. They're like a ball and chain that never comes off. So, if we want to go far, we need to pick it up and hold it close, because then it won't slow us down much. But if we try to ignore that ball, we jerk it around behind us, bruising our ankles and knocking the crap out of everything and everyone who comes close."

"You get that from fish?"

"Nope, I get it from fishing." More laughter. "I'm down here most Wednesdays. Why don't you get yourself a rod and I'll show you how it's done?" Reeling in his lure, the man packs his kit.

"That's a kind offer."

"Not kind. Someone taught me." Taking his bucket of fish in one hand and his kit and rod in the other, the man meanders down the causeway without actually saying goodbye.

"What, no story?" Simon vocalizes his disappointment to no one in particular.

"It's not my fault."

He turns and finds a boy of about nine, sitting on one of the center benches, holding a bright red kite. Simon tries to fill in the blank, "Your fault what?"

"My fault that today you decided to engage random people in conversation. Don't get me wrong. It was wonderful to witness. You should do it more often. Look at the gems he offered you. I was going to say the same thing using a kite, but fishing works just as well."

"You mean he has nothing to do with your lot?"

"Nope. Just an average citizen with above average thoughts. It's amazing what people can offer when you give them a chance. Of course with some of them, opening a conversation is like taking the wrapper off a nut bar, but you can't win them all."

"So, he really…"

"So, he'll really be here next Wednesday, and he really will teach you how to fish, which would be good for you, though not so good for the fish. That's why I like to fly kites. More importantly, there's a great ice-cream stand down from this pier. Buy me some?"

Ten minutes later, each sits with a cone.

"Okay," says the boy, "let's go over the rules again."

"Rules?"

"From last time. The rules about listening to these stories."

Simon sighs, "Don't expect a single story to offer a comprehensive world view. Don't worry about the original intent or context. Don't assume that there's any one 'correct' meaning. It's important to notice my reaction and build from there – that's where the value lies."

"Not bad, and I thought your mind was wandering in the bookstore." Popping the remaining cone into his mouth, he doesn't quite finish chewing before he starts.

———

In ancient times, there lived a woman who cared greatly about how people lived together. She found ways to draw out the best in others, even in difficult circumstances. Through her own actions, she modeled a way of life that was generous, forgiving, and just.

It also happened to be different from what those around her expected. Indeed, there were some who resented her outspoken nature and the way her actions challenged their understandings of how they should behave.

One such person lived in a house along the path by which the woman traveled every day. The old man sat on his porch, waiting for her to come into sight. At his feet he kept a pail of garbage: rinds, grounds, peels, and gristle. As she passed, he took hold of the bucket, walked to his gate, and tossed the contents in her direction. The majority fell short, but some piece always found its mark, which caused the old man to chortle with delight.

Without altering her pace, the woman would turn towards the man, smile, and brush off what could be easily removed.

Once she reached her destination, her friends would press her to change her route, or at least berate the old man for his behavior. They even offered to intervene on her behalf, but she simply laughed and noted that he had his choices and, fortunately, she had hers.

The pattern repeats for months, until the day she walks past the house and nothing happens. No garbage. No old man.

It strikes her as odd that such a committed individual would set aside a task that clearly brought him pleasure. She speaks with one of his neighbors, who informs her that he'd taken ill with no family to tend his needs.

The woman finds her way to his porch and knocks on the door. Hearing him call out from the bedroom, she enters. The rooms stand out as surprisingly neat for someone who hurls garbage.

Seeing her, the old man casts a scathing look from his bed, "No retort all these months, but as soon as I'm vulnerable, you arrive to take your revenge. You are a patient snake; I'll give you that."

She allows his comment to settle before replying, "I'm here to offer tea and a small meal. Whether you accept or not is up to you."

Each day she returns and each day the old man begrudgingly accepts her offer. He tells her why her thinking is wrong. She makes him tea and provides him with lunch.

A week later, the woman knows that her services are no longer needed when she sees from the path that the man is back, sitting on his porch, pail at his feet. She smiles.

Noticing a drop of ice cream on his shirt, the boy licks his finger, drags it across the stain and returns it to his mouth. It seems that both of us are finding it difficult to focus on the story. I offer a prompt, "So then what happened?"

"What do you mean?"

"Did he throw the garbage or not?"

"Doesn't matter."

"Doesn't matter?"

"The story's not about him. It's about her."

He seeks out another drop further down his shirt. This time he examines his finger before sticking it in his mouth, then reacts to my glare.

"Yah, I'm a bit of a test for you, aren't I?" he admits in his nine-year-old voice. "But you've got to realize that if I can throw you off your game this easily, life is going to throw you to the ground. It's like fighting in the zombie apocalypse and getting distracted by bunnies. You've got to exercise a bit of focus until it becomes second nature."

"Okay." I picture myself back on the hill, picnic basket, cookies, and all. "The story makes me think about Mateo and how he looked after the others along with his daughter. By tending to their needs, it was more than simply acting on his inclinations. By recognizing and making that choice, he was also preserving himself from becoming someone different. He made sure that potential distractions – like how those people got injured – didn't interfere with his goal of being the kind of person who does what he can to help others."

"And if you were to apply that to yourself?"

"I need my actions to line up with who I want to be. If I don't, not only am I not the person I want to be, I'm actually becoming some person I'm not intending to be."

"Tell it to me like I'm a kid."

"Fine. Let's say it's your zombie apocalypse. I need to focus on the goal of staying alive. If I get distracted by bunnies, I might end up getting bit by the undead. So, although I need to be aware of everything that's around me, including potentially edible rodents, I need to take note of which actions actually lead to life and pursue those. Part of what helps me keep that focus is the realization that not only will getting bit break my goal of staying alive, it might result in something worse, becoming something I don't want to be – a zombie."

The boy nods his head thoughtfully, "Deep." An impish grin quickly transitions into peals of laughter. I join, not sure whether he's laughing with me or at me, only knowing that it feels good. As he walks me back to my car, we take a break on the outlook so that he can fly his kite.

By the time Ailish returns from her evening run, Simon has set the table. The lighting is bright, the music lively, and the food colorful. One of her favorite dinners, the presentation of the Glory Bowl consists of separate mounds of brown rice, grated carrots, baby spinach, grated beets, slivered almonds, and a tahini dressing. Two empty bowls await the diners' personalized balance of tastes.

She unplugs her second bud and sits right down as Simon pours their water. "Dad, what's this about?"

"It's about bunnies."

"Ah, you got me a rabbit?" she teases, then becomes serious. "Wait. Tell me this isn't about the main course."

"Actually," Simon corrects, "it's about avoiding bunnies. So no worries."

"Ummm. Silly mood?"

"Silly reference. Forget about it." Simon regroups, "I have a proposal for you. I'm suggesting that every Wednesday night for the next while, we have dinner together and I'll tell you one story about your mom that you don't already know."

Somewhat stunned, it takes her a moment to respond. Her tone is more tentative than her word choice, "Sounds fantastic." She takes a sip and decides to seize the moment, "And I get to ask one question about her that you have to answer?"

"That makes me nervous, but okay."

It's more than okay. He can't remember the last time he's felt so good at the end of a day. Simon fills his bowl while searching for a starting point, "Let me tell you about the time in Seattle when your mom and I got caught in a rainstorm."

CHAPTER NINE

The pressure I'm feeling is self-inflicted. After several weeks' conversation and some pestering on her part, I told Ailish that I'd make a pattern of not working on Friday and Saturday in hopes of striking a better balance. As usual, life tends to ensue.

It's Thursday night – my new sermon night – and I'm stuck. The middle and end of the message are in place, but I'm not quite sure how to hook the congregation at the outset.

"What worked when mom was around?"

Ailish wants to help like her mom helped, which is good of her. Problem is that I don't exactly know how she helped. We'd go for a walk and an hour later I'd have that link or example or phrase for which I'd been searching all day. There was no formula, no series of steps, no secret recipe. She knew me, how I thought — the kind of honest understanding that's built as thousands of conversations erode the last vestiges of pretense.

If I don't finish the sermon this evening, it'll mean missing the days-off goal. Not a big deal in itself, but symbolically significant for both of us. Ailish is bound and determined that I make it happen, right down to sending intentionally bad motivation quotes in the middle of the day. She doesn't appreciate that after all these years, there are weeks when you don't write the sermon, you sweat it out until every word is down on paper, edited and re-edited.

But I have to give her credit. Moments ago she appeared with encouragement in the form of green tea and a ginger biscuit. If I finish the sermon tonight, she promises that she'll take me to breakfast tomorrow morning.

My cell rings. Ailish snaps it up from the table and answers as if she were my assistant, no doubt hoping to thwart unnecessary interruption. She rolls her eyes before relinquishing the phone.

Such calls are one of the realities associated with presiding at large gatherings. In this case, the caller attended a funeral for a friend's uncle the previous year. She valued the tone I set. Her mother having died suddenly, she hoped for similar assistance. Although the funeral wouldn't be held for a few weeks, her brother was in town overnight. Could they meet with me tomorrow?

I suggest 1:00 at a local coffee shop.

Call finished, I turn to Ailish. I'm still thinking about my opening line when she reviews our status, "Okay, I'll give you that tragedy and death were covered in the small print of our deal, but that doesn't get you out of finishing your sermon. No message tonight – no eggs benny tomorrow. So, drink your tea and get on with it."

Her serious expression calibrated, I counter by sticking out my tongue. She attempts to double-down on the stern look, but the corners of her mouth twitch.

Our status is clear. For her part, she's not going to make a big deal if the sermon doesn't get finished tonight. For my part, I'm not going to bed until it's done.

———

Arriving early at the coffee shop, Simon claims his favorite table. Against a wall and slightly apart from the others, it affords a modicum of privacy. Stomach already at capacity with hollandaise, he turns down the menu, opting for a double shot espresso and the local newspaper.

The first sip of the well-drawn coffee causes Simon to set down the paper and embrace the experience. Right temperature (hot but not too hot to drink right away), right crème (golden to dark brown and lasting), right aroma (rich and full without a trace of sourness), right viscosity (thicker than regular coffee but not at all syrupy), right taste (slightly bitter without being too bitter). He chuckles at the level of pleasure he's experiencing.

Entering together, the siblings are in their thirties, both impressively tall. Their hair would have been the same natural black, if not for her burgundy streak. Introductions and condolences pass quickly. By the time their coffees arrive, Simon knows he'll be here for a while.

Alena died a few days short of her sixty-first birthday. She was involved with someone at the time of her passing, but with the relationship in its infancy, her partner felt it best to step back and let her family take charge. Having been divorced for a decade, their father would attend, but felt neither the desire nor the compulsion to manage the details of her being put to rest. Given these realities and in the absence of other relations, the task fell to her children, who wanted nothing of it.

"I know it sounds terrible," the daughter confesses, "but neither of us were close to her. We'd get together every holiday and birthday; that's about it. But we wouldn't call each other out of the blue, if you get what I mean."

Simon nods, encouraging her to continue.

"Don't get us wrong, she really loved us, wanted the best for us," she adds. "Always encouraged us at school and then our careers. She really cared about how we presented ourselves to the world. It's just that she…"

"…liked to be in control," the son finishes. "Which wasn't so bad. It's not like she was an alcoholic or hit us, but she did need to direct most aspects of our lives growing up. To her, there was a way we should speak. There was a way we should dress. There was a way we should act. And in her mind, it wasn't even 'her' way. It was 'the' way, some abstract absolute."

"It was like she took all the rigor she needed to survive as a surgeon and applied it to every other aspect of her life," the daughter tags. "Once we were out of the house, Dad held on for another year."

Simon breaks into the litany, trying to ease the pace, "Sounds like Alena was pretty tough to live with."

"Living with her was only part of the problem," the daughter continues unabated. "It was her and the socials paper, her and the science lab, her and the soccer club, her and the rowing center, her and the theater production. In grade ten I made the chorus for our school musical and she complained to the director that I was being underutilized. The next year, I scored a lead, but she didn't like my costumes and kept altering them. A little lower here, more bling there. Even when the director told me to rest my voice, she kept insisting that I practice. He was furious, but she wouldn't leave it alone."

"I remember arriving at university and seeing my advisor," the son grabs the baton. "Mom insisted on coming with me to select my courses. The advisor kept directing questions to me, but mom always answered. She decided on my areas of interest, my course load, my optimal schedule. When the advisor suggested that these decisions should really be coming from me, she was livid. I was eighteen. It was so damn embarrassing."

The daughter quips, "Given that she wrote the personal paragraph for your application, maybe you should have stayed home and let her take the classes." They share a smile, finally breaking the flow.

Simon probes, looking for a way forward, "So what do you think was happening for her?"

"Mom had a pretty negative understanding of the world. People are out to rip you off. You have to fight for what you want. So, she did everything she could to control outcomes. Our lives were on a pretty tight script."

"It probably worked well for her in terms of work," the son joins. "She was a top surgeon when the pool of women wasn't very deep. You should have heard her rail when some new colleague assumed she was a nurse. She had to be larger than life when she started out."

Simon's no longer wondering how he might guide the conversation. Focusing on this glimpse of understanding into their mother's world, he tentatively steps out on the path to see where it leads, "I'm hearing that your mom's need to control situations made life hard for you, and that you have lots of examples to back up the point." He waits for nods. "Tell me. Now she's gone, what influence does she have over you?"

"I guess patterns from the past," the son offers. "I can't look in a mirror without her voice commenting on what I'm wearing."

"Yah, but now we choose whether we listen to her voice or not," admits the daughter. "And it's not actually her voice anyway. We've taken it on as part of us."

"I think you're on to something," Simon builds. "In fact, let's think of your mom's life as a story for a moment, and you are in control of what you take from it. Let's assume that no story is perfect and no single story tells us everything we need to know in the world, but each does offer some insight. I want you to set aside the very real rubbish and look for the parts that speak positively to you." Simon pauses, trying out the words before speaking them. "Here's my question. If you think of her life as a story, like you're sitting down and listening to it for the first time, what do you notice?"

In the silence that ensues, Simon wonders if he stretched too far.

The daughter nods and the son goes first. They stack their responses one on top of the other.

"She was strong."

"She was passionate."

"Knew what she wanted."

"Determined."

"Resilient."

"Okay," Simon breaks into their accelerating list, "let's pull out some examples to illustrate those words, and then we'll get to part two."

"Part two?" queries the son.

"The part where you talk about how this story of hers impacts your own lives."

Two weeks later, I'm about to close Alena's service. In a sparse but comfortable community center hall, the roughly two hundred in attendance rise for the blessing.

Earlier, the siblings stood together as they eulogized their mother. They provoked laughter when they talked about her detailed planning of family road trips down to the last restroom stop, where one had to go even if there was no need. Other stories illustrated what they most wanted to learn from their mother: her strength, her passion, and her resilience. It's with those three words of their choosing that I close the service.

After processing to the back of the room, I receive a hug from each sibling.

"You know the best thing about this whole funeral business?" says the daughter. "It's that I hold mom differently now, without having to deny how she drove me crazy."

"Yah," tags the son, "I still hear her commenting on my clothes, but now there's a new context for the nagging." He smiles. The three of us laugh. His comment rings true. The past hadn't changed, only its meaning.

I'm glad they feel this way. They worked hard with more than a few tears interrupting their natural mirth. The daughter slips me an envelope, my check. I place it in my jacket pocket with thanks. After they return to their guests, something feels forgotten until I note the absence of my usual compulsion to check the amount.

I head down the hallway in search of a washroom, only to find myself in the games room. Several groups are playing bridge; others are paired around chess and checkerboards. One lady, sitting alone in front of a crib board, eyes me closely. She looks about a thousand years old.

"My partner hasn't shown. Come play a round with me." It's not a question.

"I'm afraid that I'm part of the funeral down the hall," I apologize.

"Well, do you suppose the deceased's going to get any deader if you play one round?" I'm at a loss for words. She isn't, "In that case, come take a seat."

Shuffling and distributing the cards, her hands are surprisingly agile. She shows no mercy, exercising Muggins with glee. Once it's clear that her victory is at hand, she redirects our conversation before counting out her final hand.

"It's good what you did for Alena's children," she opens.

I suspected as much. "They did the work."

"Yes, but you also did your job, like you're starting to do again for your own kid."

"She's doing as much as me, maybe more."

"Oh for goodness sakes," the old lady spits, "take the damn compliment. Say 'thank you' so that we can get on with it."

Stunned, my words sound like a question, "Thank you."

"Wasn't so difficult, was it?"

I find wisdom in silence.

"Now, before we finish our game, it's story time. You can spare a few minutes more?"

Again, though her voice rises to mark a question, it's not. I nod anyway.

"Suddenly shy? Okay, Simon, what sort of story would you like me to tell?"

"Ah, usually you pick and I listen."

"You mean to say that after eight rounds, you can't discern what topic might be helpful at a particular juncture? Not the sharpest knife in the drawer, are you?"

I can't believe that I recently enjoyed a bookstore and ice cream as part of these conversations. This woman sets me on edge. I try to be ironic, "Sure, given the deceased's struggles, a story about control?"

"There's a good lad. Now shut up and listen."

A traveler comes across a swiftly flowing river. Standing at its edge, she admires the rapids and the eddies. The water being far too treacherous to cross unaided, she looks downstream for a bridge, but sees none. When she looks upstream, the traveler is again disappointed, but she does see an old man, leaning over the river's bank and washing his hands. Thinking that he might direct her to the nearest bridge, she starts towards him.

She barely moves when to her horror, the old man falls into the water. Immediately he's swept into the rapids. The traveler calls for help but they are alone. She looks for a long stick, an abandoned piece of rope, anything to reach the man. All she can do is watch.

The old man gets pulled under the water. She assumes that he has drowned until he pops back up further downstream. Then the old man heads straight towards a huge rock, water churning to either side. The instant before impact, he slides around the side. Over and over she watches him barely escape death.

Until, quite a distance downstream, she watches him enter an eddy before swimming safely to shore.

Running to check on his well being, she notices that he wears the robes of a monk. She inspects his head, his hands, and his feet, finding only the slightest of abrasions.

"Master," she bows, "the river is so swift. I thought you drowned when it pulled you under. Other times you narrowly missed being dashed against the rocks. No one is strong enough to fight such a force. How did you survive?"

"My child, you are right," he bows in return, "To struggle in this situation is to perish. Instead, I flow with the river. When it pulls me down, I allow it to pull me down, knowing that there will be a time when it will bring me back to the surface. When it pushes me towards the rocks, I know that the river will flow around the rocks, so I flow with the river and avoid them. I knew it would eventually bring me to a calm spot, where I could reach the shore." He squeezes some water from his robe, "Sometimes to take control, one must let go."

———

Without losing a beat, the old lady counts her final hand and pegs out. She hoots so loudly that other groups look our way, some shaking their heads.

Simon changes the subject, "So rather than fighting to tie down every detail of her and her family's life, Alena needed to let go."

"No kidding, Sherlock, but she's taking a dirt nap. The story's no use to her. You, on the other hand, could benefit from keeping it in mind."

"You're saying that I'm controlling."

"What I'm saying," she clarifies, "is that just about everyone carries the illusion that they can control far more than is possible. Sometimes it's the small things, like making sure that every single word of your sermon is typed, edited, and underlined for appropriate emphasis. Other times it's the big things, like our assumptions about how much time we have."

"That last one's been mentioned before, that I'm running out of time." Simon steels himself, "Tell me. How much longer do I have?"

"You don't even know what you're asking, but why would you want to know the answer to a question like that anyway?"

"Well, then I'd have a better idea of what to do."

"You'd have a better idea of what to do. Sure. Sure." The old lady gathers steam, "Simon, when you think of everything important in life, everything that makes it meaningful, everything that makes it worthwhile," she takes a sharp breath, "should you postpone any of it because you've got more time?"

I'm willing to hear the message, or at least, I hope I'm willing to hear the message, but I'm done with this particular messenger. While contemplating exit strategies, I'm suddenly and critically aware of why I originally ventured down the hall. Excusing myself temporarily to find the washroom, I use the time to formulate the right words by which to extricate myself without further raising her ire. I decide that I'll simply tell her that I need to resume my duties at the reception before everyone leaves.

By the time I return to the games room, she's gone. I feel doubly relieved.

Re-entering the reception, I find myself moving from conversation to conversation. I'm struck by how honored I feel to be welcomed into people's lives in this way: that the daughter and son would share deeply personal details with me, a complete stranger; that they placed trust in me as I tried to steer them through their own thoughts; and how, at the service, they were able to present their mother's story in such an honest and honoring way.

So different than how I handled Sandra's schizophrenia or the assumptions I made about Shen's contributions, or what was left unsaid about Barry's preference for work over family.

Thirty years in the game and still so much to learn.

But at least I have some time. Alena's life stands as a cautionary tale. Before leaving that first meeting in the coffee shop, her children told me how she died. The initial stroke left her incapacitated, barely able to make herself understood, completely unable to feed or clean herself. Being a surgeon, she knew exactly what was happening. Being someone who prized control, she had it ripped from her. Alena must have felt it a small mercy when the second stroke took her a week later.

I shake a last hand, exchange final hugs with the siblings, and find my way out of the community center. Sometime during the gathering, the rain stopped. On my way to the car, I don't avoid splashing in a small puddle. No time to waste.

CHAPTER TEN

"Remind me what's in this?" Simon drags his spoon through the granola, unearthing secrets. They're both sitting at the kitchen table. Bowls, mugs, everything according to routine.

"Really. Again?" sighs his daughter, sipping her coffee.

"It's the diminished capacity, the senility. Wait until you're older, then you'll understand," he laments before stumbling on an idea. "Better yet, why don't you show me how to bake it or cook it or whatever it is that you do."

Ailish shakes her head, "If you can't remember the ingredients, how are you going to remember the recipe?"

"Because I can knock it into my phone and then it'll be a permanent part of me. I could even tape the whole thing; it could go viral."

His daughter sighs. Although his outward expression is intentionally overdramatic for comedic benefit, Simon's actually quite enthused by the concept. He'd been rummaging through his mind in search of a joint project and now one ascended from the kitchen table. The more he considered the possibility, the more perfect it seemed, especially because it would center on something Ailish learned from her mom.

"Alright," she resigns, "but absolutely no video."

"No video, but I get to take still shots. Final offer."

"Deal." She changes the subject, "So who's on the roster today?"

"I'm off to see Frank this afternoon."

"Seems that you're seeing a lot more of him these last months. I know he's getting worse again, but I get the feeling that he's become more than a client for you. It's going to be hard when he dies, isn't it?" She looks for Simon's response.

"That will be a sad day for a bunch of people," he deflects, not realizing it.

"Including you," she catches his eye, offering a slight frown before getting up from the table and grabbing her bag. "Well, that's enough caffeine for me. I'm off. See you tonight, but I'll be a little late. My group's doing their long run. Love you."

Simon reaches up to receive a quick hug, "Love you, too. Be safe."

———

Perfect pairing. A shared bottle of Guinness and a plate of sliced cheese infused with the brew's deific, creamy richness. "Who needs transubstantiation?" Irreverent laughter between friends.

Frank's impossibly propped up on the right hand side of a queen bed. I'm in a round-backed, wooden chair at his side, sitting directly beside his dialysis machine. Only recently has the latter been effective enough to allow such variation in diet. That, combined with the recognition that he no longer has the time to postpone simple pleasures.

In the past, I would have spent a lot of energy regretting that we didn't meet sooner. Instead, I strive to savor.

In the moment of laughter, I scan the room, looking for signs of change. The hospice binder holds place on the wardrobe, no longer at the bottom of a stack in the kitchen. There's a little foot stand beside the bed to assist with entry and exit. And, of course, Frank is thinner, frailer — his cough only a symbolic gesture of what it would take to clear the fluid from his lungs.

But those are the only changes. A thick tome on European history sits on his bedside table, even though he can only read a few pages before his hands ache. The iPad carries the news and access to Dharma Talks. Because crosswords aren't enough, a half-finished *Jumble* awaits further attention. He's in the same bed, an act of sublime stubbornness. His wife still spends part of the night with him, something that couldn't happen if he accepted the narrower hospital version.

Most importantly, it's the same Frank. His manner is gentle and his mind brilliant.

They prepared him to miss his daughter's high school graduation. Now he's holding on for her undergrad, though he's unlikely to get that far. It's not that a single physical failing will take him. What started out as cardiac failure morphed into a litany of complications. General weakness grew precise: joints seize, muscles cramp, sleep eludes – every intervention on behalf of one symptom negated by its impact on another.

Yet, he remains gracious.

"Don't get me wrong," he tells me, "this isn't the end I had in mind, but I've had a lot of luck in my life." He goes on to talk about his wife, the time they shared in the city as a couple, the arrival of their children. Then there was his career, how unlikely doors opened with precise timing.

Some of these stories I've already heard, but I don't let on. Rather than an act of compassion, it's a kind of selfishness on my part. When a story is repeated, new details emerge. Subtle shifts alter emphasis, revealing nuances formerly missed. Besides, it's not only the telling that's different, it's my hearing. Over the past year, I've changed.

By the time he finishes his half share of the banquet, Frank tires. We talk a little more before saying goodbye.

I speak briefly with his wife to get a sense of how she's coping. We exchange a hug at the front door before I head down the steps. Strange to be leaving his house by stairs that he won't walk down again. I'm used to people dying, but I don't want Frank to go.

Making my way down the street to the car, I notice the pink blossoms on the trees. The sun catches them. The breeze teases, threatening to dislodge the delicate petals. Not one flutters onto the wide sidewalk, a very brief moment in the annual cycle. I will miss him.

Benches are interspersed among the trees. A few are empty. Two women sit on one, holding hands. A mother rests on another, her face turned to the sun, while her little guy races his car back and forth between her and the opposite arm rest. Further along, an old man wrapped in the orange robes of a Buddhist monk sits alone. I sigh and take my place beside him. We acknowledge each other with a nod, then face forward. I open.

"Subtle."

"I thought something formal was appropriate."

"When are you taking him?"

"You've forgotten the thoughts I offered on timing?"

My temper spikes, surprises me, "Screw your rationale. Tell me."

He turns to me and smiles. There's nothing mocking or malicious in his expression. His eyes wrinkle at the corners, both moved and amused. He sets my question softly aside as if it were never spoken.

We both gaze forward. He begins, "I have a story for you..."

I'm about to tell him to also screw his story, when he stops himself, and turns to face me. I don't reciprocate. Instead, I focus on over-hanging blossoms.

"This is when it matters, Simon, when life challenges us. It's the highs and the lows that reveal our core, more so than the everyday."

Several minutes of silence follow. I take a deep breath and allow it to escape, "Tell me the story."

It is well past nightfall. A servant stands at the door of the throne room. The king sits in the grand chair, arms on rests, staring without focus. His unadorned, golden crown dangles from his right hand, threatening to fall. A single torch casts shadows through the room. They are alone.

This trusted servant knew better than most the burdens carried by the king, whose decisions were the difference between justice and oppression, war and peace. He breaks the silence, "My King, what troubles you?"

The monarch raises his eyes, only now realizing his servant's presence. He lifts himself off the throne and moves to a grouping of simpler chairs by the wall, gesturing that the servant join him. "My friend, you ask of my troubles. Would you have me burden you with my thoughts?"

A smile passes between them. Each well in the other's confidence, the question and its answer reflect an earlier time, a ritual. "If you would share them with me."

Taking a breath, the king's smile fades, "With my crown comes power and responsibility to be exercised on behalf of the people – I know this." A deeper pause. "I know, as well, my shortcomings. Because of this, there are times when my confidence wanes and I hesitate when I should act, which in turn adds to my sense of failure."

The servant wants to assure his king that this is not true, but looking into the monarch's eyes, he simply nods. The king is wise, not perfect.

"But that's not all," continues the king, "Equally, there are times when I'm quite clever and receive praise, so that I grow overconfident. I'm so sure of myself that I act when I should hesitate."

Again, the servant simply nods.

"By sabotaging myself in these ways, I misuse the power and betray the responsibility accorded to my role."

After a pause, the servant responds, "So, my King, I hear two things. First, when you are losing confidence, you need assurance. And second, when you are becoming overconfident, you need to be cautioned. With these, you would be a better king."

"And without them, I should not wear this crown."

The two speak until the sun rises and the room fills with light, but still a solution eludes them. His determination undiminished, the servant proposes a way forward, "If we are without an answer, one must be found. Allow me to consult the wisest of our land."

And so with his monarch's blessing, the servant sets out across the land, seeking women and men renowned for their wisdom. With each, he shares the king's struggle. From each, he takes words of advice.

As he travels from the north to the south, from the east to the west, reaching the very borders of the territory, the burden of the task overwhelms him. Having recorded every word spoken, he now travels with boxes: boxes filled with books, books filled with pages, pages filled with words, all for his king. "But what use are these," he laments, "there is no consensus and the king can't read through all this material every time a decision is made."

Abandoning the boxes, the servant returns home. As the city appears in the distance, the taste of failure sours his mood. An ill-tempered wind rises. By the time he arrives at the gates, he cannot bring himself to enter. He sits on the ground, deriding his inability to ease the king's mind. The wind kicks dust into his face. It catches his curse and his attention. He listens as it gusts and swirls. The servant discerns a pattern within the breeze, a pattern that whispers, "This, too, shall pass."

The servant rolls the words in his mind, "Yes, it's true I've failed. But as for tomorrow and the next task, it might be different. It's not the first time I've needed to let go of my shortcomings and it won't be the last. This, too, shall pass." Somewhat comforted, he gets up and enters the gate.

Then it strikes him. The four words address half of the king's quandary. When the king feels insufficient, when he worries about failure, when he feels overwhelmed and begins to lose confidence, the four words will offer assurance.

"And," growing more excited, "these are my own words. After visiting the wisest in our land, it came down to me." Walking swiftly, proudly, he imagines how the rest of the court will react; how the king will react. The palace now in sight, the servant is overjoyed.

At this moment the still active wind gusts, again blowing dust into his eyes and provoking a curse. In the silence that follows, the words are softly repeated.

The servant stops in his tracks, "This is also true. Today I may receive praise from the court and the king, but I am still myself, shortcomings and failings intact. I should savor this moment but not let it mislead me about my own greatness. This, too, shall pass."

As the wind continues unabated, the servant realizes that the same four words address the second half of the king's quandary. When the king becomes overconfident, when he thinks too much of his own knowledge and skills, the four words will encourage caution.

The servant resumes his walk at a thoughtful pace, eventually entering the courtroom. Seeing the king on his throne, he imagines the weight that comes with the crown. Word of his return has drawn a crowd to the room. As the servant steps forward, they part. The monarch steps down from his throne, but maintains a formal distance.

"My King, I have traveled this land from the north to the south and from the east to the west. What I share with you was gifted to me by the winds." The servant pauses for a breath, "The winds gust over the highest mountains and lowest valleys, blowing through the homes of the weakest and the strongest, the youngest and the oldest, the most impoverished and the most wealthy. From their experience of our lives, the winds offer these four words: This, too, shall pass."

Members of the court begin to chatter, "It doesn't make sense. What does it mean?" But the king understands. He smiles, steps forward, and embraces his servant.

A simple, copper ring bearing the four words is struck for the king, who allows it to tarnish on his finger. Though the court doesn't notice, the message is not lost on the servant. Though the gold crown is set *aside at the end of each day, the green band never leaves the king's finger.*

The silence that holds the cleric and the monk to their bench is full. The young boy toddles off with his toy in hand and his mother in tow. Birds inspect the bench for his leftovers. The couple cross the street, chatting about blossoms. No sooner have they departed than an elderly woman parks her walker and rests in their place. Occasionally, a car defies the otherwise perfect setting, but only for a moment.

"I know that my time with Frank will pass, so I'm doing my best to savor these remaining visits. I also get the second part. I realize that when he dies, that immediate sense of loss will eventually pass." Simon searches for his point, "But that doesn't lessen the loss."

"Should it?" replies the monk.

"Well, if I take the story at face value, by being philosophical in my approach, my emotions will fall away."

"Interesting. I look at it differently." The monk turns his focus to Simon. "By being spiritual in this way, my emotions fall into place."

"What do you mean?"

"When something truly good happens, I can completely experience my sense of joy. No part of me holds back, wondering whether or when the feeling might end. I don't give energy to the anticipation of the loss, because I've already let it go. In other words, my practice does not dim the joy. Instead, it frees me to fully engage in the emotion." The monk allows time for the thought to settle in their minds and then continues, "Likewise, when something truly tragic happens, I can completely embrace my sense of sorrow. Again, I don't hold back to protect myself out of fear that I will always feel this way. I know that it will pass, so I'm able to fully experience my sadness."

"Beautiful, but easier said than done, I think," reflects Simon.

"That's why they call it a spiritual practice and not a spiritual walk in the park." He smiles, "We work at applying it consistently when the lows and highs aren't quite so extreme. Over time, we become more aware until eventually it's second nature. Even then, there are times when we struggle."

"Perhaps it's like my daughter preparing for a marathon," Simon connects. "She didn't start by running the full distance. Over time and through running partners, she built her capacity one training session at a time. Occasional injuries were already anticipated and taken in stride. Time was set aside for healing and for rest."

"Perhaps," the monk offers ambivalently.

"You don't agree?"

"I don't run marathons, so how would I know whether to agree?"

The two laugh. A few minutes later, the monk places his hand on Simon's shoulder, "It's time for me to go. Don't forget to take care of yourself as you look after Frank." The monk gets up, stretches out his back, and sets a surprisingly quick pace down the sidewalk, a gust of orange.

Simon remains on the bench, pondering his upcoming sermon. Most of the time, it's his default thought topic, though today it doesn't hold long.

His mind finds its way back to Frank. Simon ponders the story and his desire to fully enjoy the remaining time with his friend, but the other side of the equation is harder to imagine. By fully embracing the emotion, might sorrow be more meaningful and healthy in the long run? Difficult to say, but it's the sort of thing that Frank loves to discuss. Simon decides to use it as fodder for their next meeting, worthy of a Guinness.

He looks up into the blossoms, still being pulled by the gentle breeze as they catch the softer light of later day. On the branch immediately above him, one gives way. Simon follows the blossom, which floats on the air as if striving to delay its fall. Or, perhaps, it gently descends as it lets go completely. Either way, it comes to rest on the pavement at his feet. The cycle continues.

CHAPTER ELEVEN

"Simon!"

From the other side of the street, she hails him like a cab. Striding to the crosswalk, the pedestrian sign lights after she steps onto the street. Steel grey pant suit, white camisole, shoulder length hair – a study in voguish sovereignty.

"A little intense this morning?" he jibes.

"Not all days are created equal."

Her face softens, but not her pace. She points to the nearest coffee shop, orders an absurdly complicated drink, and leaves with it in hand before Simon's coffee appears. He sees her waiting outside, but she starts walking as soon as he's through the door. He jogs a few steps in order to catch her.

"I'll walk you to work," she states.

"More like a run, don't you think?"

"Perhaps you could use the exercise."

The comment strikes a nerve. He doesn't let on, "Had you let me know, I would've worn runners."

She abruptly closes the banter, "Later today you're going to be contacted about a memorial. It might be helpful for you to have a story in hand before you hear about the choices he made."

"Does the story explain his choices?" Simon finds himself a bit out of breath.

She replies pointedly without dropping pace, "To an extent, but I'd concentrate on what the story means for you."

A boy once trained under a master archer. When he first arrived at the dojo located at the forest's edge, he was clumsy and timid. Over many years of study, though, the novice grew familiar with all aspects of the art. He learned to shoot, of course, but also turned his hands to the making of his equipment. He was particularly adept at crafting a traditional bow, the yumi, splitting the bamboo and then shaping it with binding and shims. In this way, every detail of the process from the initial selection of bamboo to the final release of an arrow became second nature to the archer, now a young man.

In shooting, he surpassed the other students. He would first release one arrow into the center of the target and then let fly a second, which would split the first in two. His confidence increased, but so did his arrogance. He became dismissive of the efforts of other students and bragged about his own accomplishments. He spoke openly about having learned all there was to learn in the dojo.

Then one day, the Master, a venerable monk in his seventies, asks the young archer to join him in the dojo for a private session. Once they prepare, the Master moves the sliding doors of the wall, revealing the open grassy area with targets in the distance.

Signaling that they will share one target, the Master raises his bow, hands above his head, and then draws the bow by lowering his arms. His arrow finds the center of the target.

The young archer perfectly reflects his Master's technique, drawing his bow and releasing an arrow. It splits his Master's in two.

"My student," the Master smiles, "you have indeed learned how to control your bow. Let us go for a walk."

Taking their equipment, the two men head out of the dojo and into the forest. Intrigued at first, the young archer soon grows frustrated with the silent wandering of the old man. Finally, the monk stops at a deep chasm. A single log stretches across its width.

The Master signals for his student to wait. Taking his bow and two arrows, the old man steps onto the log and walks to its center. There, *he stands for a moment before nocking his arrow and raising the bow. Lowering his arms and drawing the string, he holds the arrow steady before its moment of release. It strikes the center of a tree, far along the other side of the chasm. He takes a breath, adjusts his feet. Nocking his second arrow and drawing the bow, he lets it fly, cleaving his first in two. The Master's face expressionless, he returns to the student, silently inviting him to shoot.*

Having watched his Master's success, the student quickly mounts the log and moves to its center. He raises his hands above his head, ready to draw his bow. Suddenly, he's aware of a wind pushing against him. Worse, the log sways gently under his feet. His eyes catch sight of the jagged rocks far beneath him. Shaking, he lets the arrow fly before finishing his draw. It falls well short of the target. Fearing for his life, he calls out, "Master!"

The old man walks out to the archer, takes his hand, and leads the student to safety. No words are exchanged during their return to the dojo.

Once they arrive and store their equipment, the Master and the young archer sit across from each other on the dojo floor.

The student laments, "Master, I am ashamed of myself."

The old man lets the words rest in the space between them. Eventually he asks, "What causes you to judge yourself in this way?"

"When I stood on the log, I missed the target entirely."

Again, the Master allows the words to sit. After a while he probes, "What did you notice when you stood on the log?"

"The wind, the movement, the rocks — my fear. My entire focus was on these."

"And this causes you to feel shame?" The old monk smiles, "Perhaps you simply have more to learn." Without articulating a lesson, the Master leaves the student to contemplate his own thoughts.

In the days that follow, the other students notice a shift in the young archer. Not only does he practice his art, he pays full attention to the words of their Master. He speaks little of his own accomplishments and over time begins to take pleasure in those of the other students. Instead of arrogance, he comes to be known for his humility, becoming a famed teacher in his own right. Eventually, the Master dies, leaving the dojo to his student.

With each new group of youth, the archer sits with them in a circle on the floor. The first words of the lesson are always the same. "It is one thing to control your bow. It is another to control your mind."

Simon and the woman continue their rapid pace in silence. Catching a breath, he asks, "Will I see you after I meet with his family?"

"Who said anything about meeting his family? But yes, I'll get back to you. This is your stop. Good luck."

She leaves Simon precisely next to the church office walkway. His administrative assistant greets him with a message from the funeral home. Could he make a 10:00 meeting?

I arrive ten minutes early for the meeting and find myself in a room just big enough to hold the oval table with its eight chairs. All the pieces are shaped from a wide-grained, dark oak. The two framed reproductions are heavy on gold frame and light on content: flowers in vases. It's an interior office, no windows.

Writing "Martin" on the top of my notepad, I scribble what I know from the funeral director: 47, cancer, high level stock broker, divorced, parents alive, eight year old daughter; represented by a friend, not family. I place a question mark beside this last point. Although a friend might accompany family members to these meetings, it's highly unusual for there to be no family present. Hopefully they're still arriving from out of town. It'll probably entail another meeting for me, but such is the business at hand.

A few minutes past the hour and the friend arrives. He's a little older than Martin and presumably stepping out of the office for our meeting. He sports a vibrant, hand painted tie to complement his warm greeting. As he sits, I catch a glimpse of equally colorful socks. He pulls out his phone and begins to tap. I think this rude until I realize that he's bringing up his notes.

"Martin was a good friend of mine," he opens. "His parents can't travel soon enough to make the initial arrangements and his ex-wife doesn't want to be involved. So, you have me as your guide."

"I appreciate the help," I reply. "It makes such a difference when the service reflects the individual who died. We can get to the details of format later. Let's start with me getting an idea of who your friend was. What can you tell me?"

"I've been giving this some thought." The friend hesitates, "Although I'm loathe to say anything negative, I think you need to know some of the unpleasant details along with the good. It'll help you navigate some of the feelings that'll be in the room. Without context, it'll be hard for you to figure out what's going on for some of us."

"How about I hold everything you say in confidence and then we can decide what'll be said when the time comes?" I offer.

He agrees and begins to sketch out his friend's life.

They met at university, sharing a few classes and the same dorm. Martin was marvelously outgoing, close to the center of any gathering he entered. Given his penchant for celebration, you'd expect his marks to suffer, but they didn't. He had real skills in working with people, the right words at the right moment. He possessed the kind of adventuresome mind that was geared for growth, always searching for the next step that would take him further up the path. The impulse carried over into his work, where he excelled as a trader, mainly because of the relationships he built.

His personal life reflected the same focus, starting with a solid relationship with his girlfriend before they married. Martin was thoughtful, considerate. Though some wondered how he'd find the time, his circle accurately predicted that he'd be a dedicated parent, never having lost his playfulness. He was the kind of guy who kept a picture of his wife and daughter on his desk. When asked about how life was going, he'd respond, 'Unreasonably well.' He meant it.

From the outside, it seemed that he had built a near ideal existence, but he couldn't sit back and enjoy it. Martin still sought that next step, that next adventure. A couple years ago, it was like his drive came unhinged from his goals.

The affair started quite innocently. She being twelve years younger, a mentorship role seemed wholly appropriate. As they got to know each other, Martin began to see that she was someone who shared his desire for the ever-expanding "next." Meetings slowly evolved from coffee to lunch to dinner. Colleagues noticed the shift in their interactions, along with the joint business trips. Eventually, only the daughter's photograph held place on his desk.

When his wife finally put the pieces together, the remains of their relationship imploded with an intensity that corresponded directly to its former strength. She hammered him for his infidelity, taking a surprisingly generous slice of his worth, along with most of their daughter's custody time.

And yet, Martin seemed mostly unfazed, wholly engaged in the life he was building with his new partner. That is, until the firm offered her a position in one of the foreign offices, which she accepted without discussion between them. She explained that this was the next logical step for her and that she wanted a clean start. No, he needn't apply for a transfer.

"Martin never let his surface crack. That wasn't his way," the friend assesses. "Instead, he became a shell. He was as smiling and talkative as ever, but you could tell that there was an emptiness behind it all."

"Did you ever talk to him about it?" I ask.

"Yes. Often. Usually, he'd beat himself with rhetorical questions. Something along the lines of 'When you build a worthwhile life and then throw it away, what does that say about you?' Then he'd move to another topic."

I nod, "Martin obviously had the skills and initiative to build a good life in the first place. What do you think happened?"

"You know, it's like watching a disaster unfold in slow motion. Without thinking about the implications, someone releases a tiny ball of snow at the top of a hill and it creates an avalanche. I don't think Martin had any idea where his decisions were taking him. It's like he narrowed his focus and blindly obeyed his impulse to set the snowball free, not thinking about how he wanted things to end up or who might get hurt. He lost sight of what was most important. Don't get me wrong, he was a great guy. I'm sure that if he had more time, he would have figured it out."

The friend cups his hands, as if forming an imaginary snowball, "It's terrible to say, but if he had to die, I almost wish the cancer took him three years ago. It would have been better for him."

―――

Once out of the funeral home, Simon sets a swift pace. The blocks pass rapidly beneath his feet. When he notices the distance covered, he wonders how much it echoes his earlier walk or whether it's more about putting some space between himself and Martin's unfortunate tale. Moments later, he's hailed.

"I'll walk you to your office."

Déjà vu, which Simon elects to end, "If you want to talk, we can stop and talk. I'm not interested in sprinting through my day." He's surprised by his own stance.

She stops and looks at him, unstated delight in her face, "There's a bench in the park down that way."

Soon the two of them find their seat in a corner lot park, shaded from the afternoon sun by young maple trees. Set back from the street, the bench offers some perspective on the coming and goings of pedestrians and cars.

"Okay, we're sitting," she states. "I told you a story and you heard about Martin. What did you notice?"

"Well, it's easy to draw some parallels. Martin reminds me of the Archer in that he has considerable skills and confidence. Like splitting his own arrow in two, Martin builds a great life for himself on all fronts."

"Until..." she leads.

"Until he focuses on his impulse for adventure, for change." Simon frowns, then qualifies, "The impulse isn't wrong in itself, but it can't be the only focus. Like when the Archer becomes aware of the wind and the movement and the rocks, it's not that he shouldn't pay attention to these realities. He needs to be aware and at the same time measured in his response. Because they aren't, both characters miss their own goals."

"The difference being?"

"That the Archer had the chance to reflect and rebuild, whereas Martin didn't have the benefit of time," Simon falls into a silence that his companion allows to extend. They watch the flow of people.

As the cars and pedestrians move in and out of view, he continues, "I realize he tore apart his world, but I wish he had time to put it back together."

"There is a saying, 'the glass is already broken.' Do you know what it means?"

"Impermanence. All things end."

"Yes, and more." She turns to Simon, gesturing as she speaks, "You lift a glass in your hand, admiring how it holds the water or reflects the light or rings when you tap its edge. At the same time, you know that it is already broken. Someday the wind or my elbow will knock it to the ground, leaving it shattered. When it breaks, it comes as no surprise. Until it breaks, I more deeply appreciate its worth and my time with it."

They sit in silence for some time before Simon finally shares the thought passing through his mind, "My life is already broken."

"Yes," she confirms, as if having waited patiently for him to arrive at this conclusion. "Your life is already broken."

Arriving home, I find Ailish in the kitchen. Tie-died apron attached and Franti on the stereo, she's already started the chicken and pepper risotto, this evening's cooking project. It took me a while to master the granola, sending two batches over the edge from golden brown to what she described as dark and crispy. Once I got the hang of it, we began to expand our efforts.

"I've already been stirring for ten minutes, where have you been?" she interrogates.

"Waiting for you to finish making dinner."

"Fat chance. I left you the raw chicken to skin, slice, and skillet," she pauses to see whether I notice.

"How long have you been practicing the alliteration?"

"Ten minutes." That smile.

I take my place as sous and work on the chicken. She hates the viscous feel of it, but I don't mind. In the background of our banter, my mind churns through the day. I succumb to the growing realization that like the Archer and Martin, I lost my way. I disconnected from what was most important and my focus grew skewed. A tendency to worry about other people's opinions became a fixation. My self-talk became cynical and quick to judge. Most painfully, I blamed my daughter for our struggles when I was pretty much an absent parent.

The death of a spouse can do that to you, but it's no excuse.

By some grace, I've been allotted the opportunity to reflect and regroup. It'll take time, I know. Hopefully, I'll get more of a chance than poor Martin. With all the talk about running out of time, one has to wonder, but even if my glass breaks now, at least I've reconnected; at least I'm heading in the right direction. There's a certain peace in that knowledge, especially when it comes to Ailish. Of course, I'd rather postpone the inevitable, but the destiny of that glass isn't fully within my control.

"Are you going to meditate on the chicken or cook it?" she blasts into my thought process.

"So I'm in Hell's Kitchen now?"

"Only if I finish stirring before you have the bird ready."

I threaten her with my chicken-greased hands. She squeals, but doesn't stop stirring. I ask her about her day. We talk politics. Because it's a Wednesday, I share a story about her mom. Dinner is only slightly marred by my overdone chicken.

I savor.

CHAPTER TWELVE

A season passes, but Thursday nights remain the same for Simon. If Friday and Saturday are to be days of relative rest, the sermon is due.

At the kitchen table, books open, papers strewn, Simon faces off against his deadline. Though a much friendlier affair than his former Saturday night ritual, it exacts a toll. Fortunately, this particular message wants to write itself. He might well be finished before 10:00, which means that a reward scotch awaits the final product. Though the topic at hand is serious, Simon smiles with satisfaction.

While setting down his concluding thoughts, he hears the doorbell. On occasion, Ailish forgets her key. Trying not to lose his train, he walks quickly down the hall and throws the deadbolt before rushing back to his laptop.

Simon's already tapping when the bell sounds again. "It's unlocked!" he shouts. Only a few more sentences to go.

His concentration breaks on the third ring. Pushing his chair from the table, he stomps down the hallway, not angry, but certainly ready to feign upset. If she didn't wear the earbuds while running, she'd hear a whole lot better. Reaching the door, he swings it open without a word and sets back down the hall.

Halfway down the corridor, something seems amiss. He shifts his attention back to the door, where two police officers stand.

The woman asks, "Are you Reverend Murray, father of Ailish Murray?"

"Yes," then shakes his head with the growing realization. He swallows.

"I'm very sorry. Could we please sit down?" The officer knows the protocol. So does Simon.

"I'd prefer to stand," he counters, steeling himself. "What's happened to her?"

"Are you sure you won't sit?"

"I'll stand."

She checks his resolve and moves to the next stage, "We received a call that a young woman collapsed while running. An ambulance was called, but she was already gone." She allows him to absorb before continuing, "She was carrying her driver's license. We're very sorry, sir, the woman was your daughter."

Simon turns, walks back to the kitchen, and slowly sits in his chair. The second officer closes the front door, while the first follows him to the table.

"May I take a seat," she asks, hand already on the back of a chair. He nods. Simon stares at the screen, not reading a word.

After a few minutes of silence, she recites her next line, "Reverend Murray," her voice calm, "can we contact someone for you, a friend or family member who can be with you?"

"Is she in the morgue at the hospital?" his voice flat.

"Yes."

"Please take me there." Rational, collected, "I don't think I should drive."

Unreal. Sitting in the back seat of the cruiser, listening to the tick of the indicator before turning each corner. One street lamp casts light until the next one takes over. We wait at a red light even though cars aren't passing through the intersection, the stillness of the moment broken by the intermittent squawk of the radio, signaling an accident or an incident; the merciful silence of the officers, my blurred vision. Sporadic tears form, slide down my cheek, drip somewhere. I stare without focus.

My daughter.

We made dinner last night, slices of sourdough spread with pesto sauce and topped with sliced heritage tomatoes and bocconcini, all broiled before being splashed with balsamic vinegar. I gave her hell for the way she held the knife. Told her that I didn't want blood spoiling the beautiful white of the cheese. She said that she'd be sure to injure herself while cutting tomatoes. That way the color wouldn't offend.

I can smell the basil and the vinegar. I hear her laughter, see her smile.

We cross the bridge. The downtown core comes into view. So many lights. Apartments stacked on top of one another. For the people inside, simply another day. Watch a bit of television. Turn off the lights. Go to sleep. Wake up. Everyone will be there.

Last night in the midst of preparing dinner, I told her another story about her mom, how she loved to swim in the ocean. Not in some pale blue Mediterranean bath, but off the West Coast of Vancouver Island. Ailish and I would stay on the beach, building the ultimate sandcastle, while her mom waded into the waves, eventually diving into the brine. Whereas the surfers all wore wetsuits, she braved the cold. Coming out, her hands were wrinkled and incredibly white, except for the knuckles, which seemed so red in contrast. When you were old enough, she took you into the waves on her shoulders, crouching down and leaping up, always keeping your head above the water. You screamed and then laughed with the breaking of each wave.

The two of you.

Hearing my name, I see that the cruiser is parked. The officer's holding open the door for me. Once we enter the hospital, another person joins us. I've worked with her before, victims' services. My care transferred, the officer again offers her condolences and walks back into the night with her partner.

I assure my new companion that I know what to expect and that she doesn't have to prepare me. I consider telling her to go, but she has her own protocols to follow. It must be odd for her, being led to the morgue rather than doing the leading. It's not like the way is marked with one of those lines drawn on the wall or floor. You have to know where to find it. Even the sign beside the door is nothing more than a tiny plaque.

Walking down long corridors, I'm struck by how many people are alive in the hospital. So few are dead at any particular moment.

As we come to the final door, the slowness with which I open it reminds me of sneaking into Ailish's room when she was three or four years old, checking to see if she was actually asleep in her bed. At one point it seemed that every second night I'd find her passed out with her stuffies or a picture book. I became an expert at scooping her from the floor and laying her in bed, creatively balancing her menagerie along the edges. It always surprised me, how I'd get caught up in that moment, simply watching her sleep. Satisfied that she was indeed out for the night, I'd end the ritual by kissing her on the forehead.

She's covered head to toe by a sheet. I nod to the attendant. He reveals her face.

Simon gently shifts strands of his daughter's hair, touches the side of her face. Pulling the sheet further back, he finds Ailish's hand and holds it in his own. A chair appears and he sits. Placing his other hand on her shoulder, he leans forward, burying his face against her. Only a few phrases are perceptible: love you, proud of you, tell mom I miss her. This mantra he repeats as an hour ticks away.

Standing, he leans over and kisses her forehead before tucking the sheet. One more look. Another kiss. Accepting an arm around his waist, he's guided away from her face and back down the corridors.

Finding himself in a small meeting room with chairs set off by a side table, Simon's not sure how or when he arrived. Looking more closely, he recognizes the setting and knows that a doctor will be along to explain what can be explained. They'll allow enough time for him to collect himself. Another hour passes, neither slowly nor quickly.

The doctor arrives in scrubs, opening with condolences. Their best assessment is that his daughter suffered a sudden cardiac arrest, but an autopsy would confirm. Unlike a regular heart attack, this failure was likely caused by a congenital defect. There would have been nothing the paramedics could offer and her passing was probably instant. For that matter, there likely wasn't a sign of any problem until it was over. With these situations, it's only a matter of time before the electrical system malfunctions.

As he's between surgeries, the doctor repeats his condolences and departs, leaving Simon with the woman from victims' services. She asks whether she can call a family member. She asks if she can contact a friend. She asks if she can arrange a ride home.

Simon thanks her for her kindness and leaves the room. He'll walk home. He's free to do so. Even if it takes the night, no one will wonder what's delayed him.

She presses that he really should call someone, then relents. After another round of condolences, Simon knows he's at his limit. As the doors slide open to the night air, his pace quickens, but he does not run.

It's cold. I move swiftly, muttering under my breath, anger and despair condensing into a solid cloud as the words leave my lips. I've been walking for hours.

This is so wrong. She was only nineteen, barely an adult. Smart. Kind. Resilient. Direct. Lousy with a knife but fantastic with words. So much to say. Now silent.

Of all the people to suffer a heart attack or cardiac arrest or whatever the hell it was. She was training for a fucking marathon, not binging on poutine. This was a mistake. Didn't deserve. Not the right person.

More wisps of cloud. Thoughts loop.

All so wrong. She was nineteen, hardly an adult. Kind. Smart. Resilient...

―

Needing a place to rest and warm himself, Simon steps into an all-night diner. The waitress, unnaturally cheerful for the middle of the night, leads him to a booth. Closer to the entrance, a group of older teens loudly exchange jokes as their 24-hour breakfasts sop up the alcohol in their systems. Another booth holds a couple who lean toward each other, speaking softly. Three other clients sit separately, likely shift workers on their break. One of them reads a newspaper, examining every inch of column.

The waitress arrives for Simon's order. He asks if it would be okay to only have a coffee. With a hint of disappointment, she says it's no problem. Looking at him more closely, she quickly recovers. In fact, if he's willing to wait, she'll start a fresh pot.

Simon watches the teenagers, wondering whether Ailish had the experience of partying with friends until dawn. He could see her sitting among them. Not exactly eavesdropping given the volume, Simon pegs the group as university students, their current debate fueled by a poli-sci course. He'd pity anyone who tried to best her rhetorical skills.

The couple still lean across their table. Although there had been partners, Ailish avoided over-sharing on that front. Simon wonders whether this kind of intimacy was something she experienced. Probably. Hopefully.

Steam rises from the cup placed before him. A small napkin rests between cup and saucer in event of spills. The waitress asks if there's anything else. Simon shakes his head.

She does not leave. Instead, she slides into the seat across from him.

"Whatever happened to you, I'm sorry," she starts.

"Thanks, but I'm alright," he responds.

"No. I know what 'alright' looks like and you're not a match. Something's happened and you've chosen not to go to family or friends so you've wandered into this place for some human contact."

"I came in for a coffee."

"You can stick with that story," she overrides his answer, "or you can tell me what happened."

Simon finds himself oddly disarmed. He relents, "A friend of mine has been pushing me to share more with people, but I don't think you want the burden of this thought."

"Try me."

"Okay, if you're set on knowing." He takes a breath, "My daughter died. I'm walking home, but I don't want to get there. I don't want to arrive with her not there."

"You poor soul," she reaches across the table and takes his hand. Simon begins to cry. The waitress shifts over to his side of the booth and places an arm over his shoulders. She says nothing for the longest time. When the teens are ready to leave, she motions towards the kitchen, so that the chef takes their money. Dusting flour from his hands, he steps out from behind the counter to check on the other patrons. This isn't the first time she's been waylaid by a visitor.

―――

She allows me to cry myself out, then refreshes my coffee. I ask how she knew what I needed even when I didn't. She answers that we all have our stories, but tonight is for mine, not hers.

When it feels time to leave, I surprise myself by offering a hug, which she accepts. I leave a big tip, but it feels crass. Tomorrow, I'll drop off flowers as a thank you, but for now, I'm exhausted and prepared to go home.

Once outside, the cold bites into me. As I walk, I'm more aware of what's around me. The first signs of morning light obscure the stars. More cars find their way along the road. The occasional, bundled cyclist flows along the edge. Someone with his dog, out for a pre-morning jaunt. After a few blocks, I notice an oncoming cab, which I flag. In no time, I'm standing in front of my home, keys in hand.

Before walking to the door, I'm struck by the notion that there's something I must do. Watching my breath as I exhale, I'm aware that somewhere in this horror, there's a decision I can make, a path I can choose.

Up until this night, Ailish was nothing less than fully alive. I should be the same.

I find the correct key and turn the lock. Pushing open the door, I know that her room is down the hall to the left. She will not be there. I have already tucked her sheets and kissed her forehead. She is gone.

And I will not hold back on my grief. This, too, shall pass.

CHAPTER THIRTEEN

It's been three months and two batches of granola. Time for another, I set the oven to 375.

I prefer to prep the ingredients beforehand, each measured into one of nine appropriately sized, white bowls. The largest holds four cups of quick oats. The second, two cups of rolled oats. Seven smaller bowls contain a cup each of coconut, chopped pecans, toasted sunflower seeds, toasted pumpkin seeds, cranberries, raisins, and chopped apricots. All the colors and textures, combined with the orderly way I place them on the counter, seem like an end in themselves – all the intentionality of a Zen garden.

An act of meditation.

So different from what I've been offering as advice to the bereaved for the last three decades, a procedural road map, based on what I was taught back in the days when Kubler-Ross owned grief theory. I'd tell mourners exactly what to expect with each stage representing another signpost toward recovery. There would be initial *denial*, followed by *anger* at the unfairness of it all. Eventually the anger would morph into *bargaining*. With the realization that the physical or existential haggling bears no fruit, the bereaved could expect some degree of *depression*. Because this indicates that the person now understands the reality of their loss, the ground would be set for the final stage, *acceptance*, a readiness to move on with life. I used the same map when my own wife died, forcing myself along the path, one stage at a time, conjuring up appropriate emotions, signaling all was well to those around me and myself.

Not this time.

I combine all the ingredients, except the fruit, emptying the bowls into a roasting pan. Mixing the ingredients thoroughly, I sprinkle three teaspoons of cinnamon over the amalgam. Having melted a cup of butter in a separate saucepan, I add a half-cup of honey, before drizzling the syrupy liquid over the granola. Stirring to ensure that everything is well coated, it's ready for 25 minutes in the oven.

This time I allow the ebb and flow of different emotions to wash over and around me without interference or judgement. Not an easy or tidy discipline. Like falling into rapids, there's a real desire to seize control and fight against the current.

Yet now that I notice the thoughts that accompany the mix of emotions, I'm better able to release myself to them. In some ways, grief and gratitude exist as two sides of the same coin – the experience of one makes the reality of the other more meaningful.

Her memorial was like that.

I organized the service to proceed unannounced, so that once people were welcomed, I could take my seat among the pews. A good deal of the planning happened online, so not every face was familiar. One of her friends opened with a prayer he'd written. A companion from university shared a story that captured Ailish more closely than I imagined possible, provoking laughter and tears. An old friend talked about our family of three in the early days. The picture he painted was equally wonderful and unbearable.

A cousin with whom she'd connected on Facebook flew into town so that she could sing "Good Riddance." She talked about how at first she felt cheated because she had only just gotten to know Ailish, and yet she could easily have missed her entirely, given the vagaries of life. One of the first things they discovered was a common love of Green Day. By the time she finished her song, we were all softly backing the chorus.

Another friend from university talked about Ailish's fondness for Rumi. Apparently, one poem in particular spoke to my daughter, perhaps because of her mother's death. Ailish stuck it to her mirror as a touchstone. But when this friend was going through a particularly tough time, Ailish pulled it from the glass and told the friend to keep it. Holding the small scrap of paper, she read:

> *This being human is a guest house.*
> *Every morning a new arrival.*
>
> *A joy, a depression, a meanness,*
> *some momentary awareness comes*
> *as an unexpected visitor.*
>
> *Welcome and entertain them all!*
>
> *Even if they're a crowd of sorrows,*
> *who violently sweep your house empty of its furniture,*
> *still treat each guest honorably.*
>
> *He may be clearing you out for some new delight.*
>
> *The dark thought, the shame, the malice,*
> *meet them at the door laughing, and invite them in.*
>
> *Be grateful for whoever comes,*
> *because each has been sent as a guide from beyond.*

As with all the others, this friend walked up to me once she had finished and I stood to receive her hug. As we embraced, she pressed the poem into my hand. She whispered that Ailish would feel it's for my mirror now. I held the paper as if it were delicate papyrus. It bore my daughter's nearly illegible printing.

When the time came to close, I requested that we sing "What a Wonderful World" somewhat defiantly, not because we felt wonderful at that moment, but because what we shared with my daughter was wonderful. It still rings in my ears.

The buzzer sounds. I take the granola out of the oven and stir it thoroughly. Ailish was adamant that if I missed this step, I'd accomplish nothing more than a burnt offering layered over raw grains. As instructed, I pay particular attention to stirring up the corners. Satisfied with the outcome, I set the pan back in the oven for another 25 minutes.

What amazed me was the number of old friends who attended, people whom I'd not seen since my wife died. I had no need for them at that time – no need for anything that I associated too closely with her. I thought they'd all moved on with their lives, but the way they talked, it was like they were waiting for me.

And they're a little obvious in their covert plotting. Once they realized that I was open to reconnecting, different members of the collective "happened" to call at surprisingly regular intervals, independently pulling me out for coffee or a meal. Though an appalling example of a clandestine operation, I played along and loved them for it. Nights of cards, politics, philosophy, and laughter.

When it became clear that I was finding my way forward, albeit tenuously, they began to catch me up on their own lives. Grandchildren and divorce and cancer and sojourns — all the joys and challenges that breath affords. In these quieter moments, I find that I'm not alone in my tears.

The second buzzer. As I open the oven door, the kitchen fills with the smell of warmed oats and cinnamon. It's the requisite dark golden brown. Placing the pan on the stovetop, I pour in the final cups of cranberries, raisins, and chopped apricots. Mixing it together, I leave it to cool. What it needs now is time.

———

Well ahead of his Thursday deadline, Simon sets up shop in the corner of his latest, favorite café. The number of people moving in and out on a Tuesday afternoon might astonish some, but those dedicated to the quest for a perfect espresso understand.

He moves through the ritual of inspecting and savoring the small but exceptionally well-drawn ration of caffeine. If only his writing were so well formed. He alternately enters and deletes the same sentence, getting nowhere.

Seeking inspiration, he scans the crowd. He spots a woman in her thirties unfolding a white cane. As she stands to leave, Simon determines her path of least resistance through the crowd. She's going to have a tough time reaching the exit unless someone helps.

Cutting through the assembled crowd, Simon greets her, "Excuse me, are you looking for the door?"

"Actually," she states, "I'm not *looking* for anything." Other than a slight emphasis on the adverb, there's no inflection in her voice. Simon doesn't know whether she's upset or having him on. Unreadable.

Erring on the side of caution, he takes a second to screen his next statement before giving it voice, "Sorry. I meant to ask whether you're trying to leave. There's a large line-up at the moment. I'm happy to help you through, if you want."

"Well," she confesses, "I'm not really looking to leave. I was rather hoping that you'd find me. It's been a while, Simon."

She's smiling, but can't see that I'm not.

I haven't heard from her since the month before Ailish died. That makes it four months without a single word.

Almost two years of popping into my life, happily offering commentary on all manner of death and dying, and then suddenly gone without a trace. Gone when it's my daughter in the morgue, when it's Ailish on that table.

I wrestle with my anger. I want to tell her to leave me alone, to get out of my life.

At the same time, I want to talk to her. I need to talk to her.

So I split the difference.

"Where the hell have you been?" Simon sits rigidly in his chair.

"Good to hear your voice, too," she deflects, as if suddenly aware of his mood.

"Some friend," he renders the verdict.

"I don't think I claimed to be that kind of friend," she redirects.

"So why appear now?"

"It seemed long enough," she's calm. Matter-of-fact.

"Long enough for what?"

"Long enough for you to choose a path. Long enough to figure this out for yourself."

"And I couldn't have done so with you around?"

"For a story to be meaningful, it must stand on its own. Otherwise, it's about the messenger, not the message. You know this."

What Simon doesn't know is whether the concern in her voice is for him at the loss of his daughter or for his inability to keep a life philosophy intact. It adds to his irritation, "So I'm supposed to accept the fact that you buggered off when it counted."

Impatience slips into her voice, "Of course you're supposed to accept the fact. It happened. The real question is whether you're willing to let go of your anger."

"If that's an apology, you're not very good at it."

"Okay, Simon," she takes a breath, "I'm sorry I didn't tell you that I'd be gone, and I'm sorry for not apologizing as soon as you spoke to me." She waits for her words to take hold.

Silence passes between them. Sightless, she slides her hand across the table, palm upwards. A moment later, Simon places his hand over hers. She squeezes.

Though not at ease, they are back on familiar ground.

———

As I order another round of espressos, I cast an eye back to the table. I'm not happy with her, but I know that ours is an unusual arrangement. I find myself lingering a little longer at the counter than necessary. It's only when I realize that the cooling drinks will give me away that I finally return to my seat. She doesn't comment on how long it took.

"You've developed quite a community around yourself," she prompts, her voice cautious.

Striving to shift my attitude, I smile, "Turns out that people can be quite lenient in their standards."

"What's it like to be back with them?"

"I'd rather have Ailish."

"You make it sound like a zero-sum situation. She never kept you away from your friends. You need to own that decision."

I accept her insight without comment. She's right, but I'm not ready to declare my culpability. It's one of the pieces that I've yet to sort. My community didn't abandon me – I abandoned them, which wasn't good for me or Ailish.

After allowing me time to ponder, she continues, "Seeing as you've decided to invest yourself more broadly, I have a story for you."

Anticipating this moment, I flatly respond, "If you must."

It's my turn to be unreadable. I'm sure that part of my tone stems from residual anger, but the dominant part rests squarely on a desire for the banter and relationship we enjoyed in the past. Truth be told, I miss the stories.

Judging by her overstated sigh, she knows it's more about the latter.

Once, there was a monastery. In the far past, it had been a famous pilgrimage site. People from afar would wind their way through the wilderness to enter its simple but beautifully built doors. Like the entrance, the whole complex reflected an understated elegance. The food grown by the monks provided fodder for exquisite meals and their singing raised the spirits of all who entered. Visitors felt so uplifted by the care and prayers they received, word spread to other young men, who left the wider world to join the order.

But as with all things, the season changed. New pilgrimages caught the attention of travelers. Soon the number of visitors slowed to a trickle and no young monks joined the order. As the men grew older and their revenues dwindled, the monastery fell into disrepair. The monks, who once lifted the spirits of travelers, now found themselves worn and deflated. They grumbled about their lot and each other.

No one felt the weight of the situation more than the Abbot. Charged with the welfare of the monks, he began to wonder whether it was time to close the monastery doors and disperse.

One evening, the Abbot calls the monks to the dining hall. Making plain their situation, he asks whether their prayers had inspired any new insights. Scanning the room, all the brothers shake their heads, but one. The eldest of the monks speaks slowly, "I wonder," he posits, "the Rabbi in the Woods, perhaps he would have a word of wisdom for us."

Now the Abbot had never set eyes on the Rabbi in the Woods, but he was willing to follow whatever directions the old monk could offer. The next morning he sets off, traveling on paths that rarely felt the passing of a human foot.

After two days travel, he comes upon a small cabin, no more than a hut. Cold and damp, he hopes that the smoke rising from its chimney means that a warm fire awaits. The door opens and he's ushered into a chair beside a small, crackling stove. As if having waited for his arrival, the Rabbi places a cup of hot tea in his hands and a warm blanket over his shoulders before adding the final touches to that night's soup and slicing through a rough loaf of bread.

Sitting at the table after their meal, the Rabbi asks, "My dear Abbot, what has brought you to my door?"

Before the answer leaves the Abbot's lips, tears form in his eyes. He shares his frustration and fears, disclosing both the monastery's coveted past and its sad present. At the end of it all, he lays his hands palms upwards on the table, "My Rabbi, do you have a teaching for us?"

The Rabbi strokes his forehead, as if coaxing a thought. "I do have a teaching, my Abbot, but I can only state it once and you can only repeat it once. We cannot discuss it further. After we each share the message, it cannot be spoken again. Do you understand?" The Abbot nods.

Reaching across the table, the Rabbi places his hands over the Abbot's, holding his wrists. He takes a breath and declares, "The Messiah is among you!"

After a period of silence, the two men slowly build a new conversation, careful to say nothing of the Rabbi's message. They talk late into the night.

His mind so filled with wonder at the teaching, the Abbot struggles to sleep before the long journey back to the monastery. He feels grateful that his role is to simply relay the message, nothing more. The next morning, the Rabbi sends him home with a loaf of bread and his blessing.

Two days later, the Abbot arrives at the monastery. The door swings open before he has a chance to knock. Clearly the monks have been awaiting his return. He tells them that once they have broken bread, he will tell them all that the Rabbi disclosed.

They gather in the great hall. Placing his hand on the shoulder of the eldest monk, the Abbot tells them that the Rabbi in the Woods indeed offered a lesson. He could speak the words once, but then there would be no further discussion. The monks agree to the terms.

The Abbot tells them, "The Messiah is among us!"

The monks are filled with wonder. What does this mean? Is Brother Jerome the Messiah? Brother Francis? Some even wonder, am I the Messiah?

Because they agreed to not discuss these thoughts, they could only act upon them. With the passing of the days, each monk grew in his ability to be kind and generous to the others. Soon the joy they shared as a community was no longer limited by the state of their surroundings. When travelers did visit, they were astounded by the love exhibited among the monks. Word spread and the monastery once again found itself a pilgrimage site. The buildings were restored, young men sought to join the community, and many people's spirits were once again lifted by the monks' example.

And the path between the monastery of the Abbot and the hut of the Rabbi became well-worn as the friends continued their journey together.

Simon sticks a finger into his cup to claim the last of the crème, "Do you think that people change their behavior based on words?"

"I'm not very keen on your question," she takes a sip, only half way through her coffee.

"Why?"

"It's too complex a question to answer with 'yes' or 'no.' You haven't left open the possibility of responses that aren't absolutes."

"Okay," Simon regroups. "To what degree do people change their behavior based on words?"

"Uh-uh. Still don't like it. Too big a leap." She expands, "You're framing it as a mechanistic reaction."

"Wow. Here's a closed question," the edge back in his voice. "Are you trying to be a pain?"

"No."

Silence. Simon considers his options. Somewhere at the back of his mind, he realizes why it was good that she stayed away for a bit. It might still be too soon.

Frayed at the edges, but wanting her response, he steadies himself and tries again, "To what degree can words influence people's behavior?"

"That's a much better question," she declares before volleying it back. "What's your answer?"

"I was asking you."

"I know."

Frustration. Another long pause. Another decision point. "In the story, the one phrase inspires everyone to radically change, but I'm not buying that life works that way."

"That's okay," she assures, "I'm not selling that life works that way."

"But you're telling all these stories with wonderfully tidy endings."

She takes a breath, "There's nothing wrong with these stories having tidy endings because they aren't simplistic instruction manuals for life. That's not their job. The purpose of these stories is to tap into how we choose to look at the world. Good stories remind us of things we already know to be true. Great stories draw out from us new discoveries of things that are true."

Somewhat belligerently, Simon asserts, "Clear as mud. I'm going to need an example."

"Okaay," she draws out the second syllable to let him know that she's received the message. "The last story isn't arguing that everything will be dandy in our community if someone declares that the Messiah is among us." She takes a sip, "Instead, the story reminds us that our lives are shaped by how we hold others and ourselves." Collecting crème with her finger, she continues, "At some level, all of us know this to be true. All the story does is draw out that truth in a way that makes it memorable so that we're more likely to practice the lesson." She punctuates this last point by cleaning her finger.

"Yes, but how likely? We're back to my question. To what degree does all this impact actual behavior?" challenges Simon.

"You're in a better position to answer than me."

"Nice try."

She nudges, "Think of where you were when we began and where you are now. What do you notice?"

"A whole lot of things have happened to get me where I am now."

"Yes," she continues, "and I'll wager that you've used the stories as a reference point on who you are and how you're approaching life – not because they hold simplistic answers in themselves, but because they gave voice to something deeper within you."

Eager to trump her point, he reminds, "Maybe my deeper thinking was stirred by other factors. It didn't hurt to be warned that I don't have much time."

She corrects, "Didn't have much time."

"What do you mean, didn't?" he's confused by the correction. "I'm still here."

"Ailish isn't."

She can't see his expression, but nonetheless allows him a moment before holding out her right hand, this time toward his face. A few more seconds pass before he moves slightly so that her hand cups his cheek. She feels a tear pass between his face and her palm. Time slows. Pieces falling into place.

When he nods, she withdraws her hand, "I know it's hard."

She lets her words sit before continuing, "Remember when we were talking about Frank. It's how we experience our highest and lowest moments that best reveal our core. All the stories, all the practice. This is when it matters."

Simon steadies himself with a breath before wiping his eyes, "Keep going."

"Imagine who you were with Ailish when you began working with the stories and who you were in your relationship when she died. Nobody would pretend that your relationship with her was tidy or perfect in the end, but if you take a look, there's probably enough there to answer your question. You already know the impact these stories offer for those who make it their practice to use them."

Simon nods his head, but then remembers that she cannot see him. He clears his throat, "I hear you."

She leans forward in her chair, bridging the gap, "And it's not a question of having more time or less time. It's about what you do with the time you have – what you're doing now. The answer to your question comes down to this, Simon. What difference do you notice in yourself?"

CHAPTER FOURTEEN

Another Wednesday morning. Light drizzle. Simon walks along the pier, two coffees in hand. No tourists today, but three people have lines in the water. A couple in vibrant, matching raingear stand together at the end. The third resets his line from the side. Simon walks in his direction and places one of the steaming drinks on the ledge. When the man nods to acknowledge the gift, water drips from his Tilley hat.

They share a moment of silence as the man takes his first few sips. Simon checks the white bucket at his feet for the day's catch before continuing to drink his own.

"I thought they were supposed to bite more in the rain," Simon teases.

"I'm sure they do. Just not my lure," his weathered face allows a slight smile.

"Why don't you change your lure?"

"Well then I might catch more fish."

Simon keeps the banter flowing, "Isn't catching fish the whole idea?"

"Nope. Fishing is the whole idea. Catching fish is a necessary nuisance."

"Then why not give up the rod and simply enjoy the view."

"Doesn't feel right. Should be doing something."

"Like not catching fish."

"If I'm lucky."

They return to their coffees, amused but not needing to laugh. Simon never took up a rod, but the two of them fish for hours in each other's company without saying a word, sharing most of their common experience in silence. They track the progress of a wooden sloop down the strait or spot an otter unusually far from shore or catch site of an eagle being hassled by crows. On a day like today, the action of the drizzle on the surface of the ocean itself is mesmerizing.

Although he might talk about his sense of loss with other friends, Simon does most of his grieving here. His Tilley clad friend offers an ideal environment, combining room for silent contemplation with the presence of a grounded companion.

It was on this pier that he first glimpsed the other side of the coin – his gratitude. Gradually, it's come to dominate his thoughts, particularly after realizing the magnitude of the gift he'd received in having rebuilt his relationship with Ailish before her death. Even when a wave of sorrow takes him, the emotion no longer overwhelms as it once did. Rumi makes more sense now. When he's ready to set the wave aside, Simon focuses on recalling specific moments that capture what he and his daughter shared together. These memories he builds with more and more detail until there's only room in the frame for gratitude. Almost.

He knows he's a work in progress. And a part of him still wants to feel the sting.

The drizzle passes and the sky begins to clear. The surface of the water returns to normal patterns. "Well," concludes his companion, "I was going to pack it in, but if we're going to keep fishing, you're going to need to get us another coffee."

Simon sets off down the pier.

His other routine on these visits has been to cement the wisdom stories in his mind. Where they were vivid on first hearing, parts had already fallen away. He took to jotting them down as the bits and pieces came together. On the pier, he'd test his memory, retelling them to himself until he experienced the story lines unfolding naturally. By adding nuances to the narrative, they became his own.

Once the originals were secure, he started to search for more. At first, he leafed through the philosophy and religion sections of favorite bookstores, but soon discovered what could be found in the children's area. This felt wrong, as if someone might think less of him for reading material devoid of footnotes. His first visit to a specialty bookstore for children actually had him looking over his shoulder as he entered. Fortunately, he chose to laugh at himself and bury his ego. Now, when time and commitments allow, he camps out on the floor with a stack, hoping to find one that might work for a Sunday morning or for himself.

As he walks back with the coffees in the midst of his contemplations, the sun peeks out from between the clouds. Simon's taken by the realization that a few years ago, he wouldn't be caught sitting on the floor of a children's bookstore or standing on the pier for hours watching someone fish. Yet now he couldn't imagine not doing these things. Somehow, life was becoming richer, despite it all.

Placing the steaming drink on the ledge, he checks the white bucket. Hardly believing his eyes, he taps his companion on the shoulder, smiles, and points to the salmon.

The companion raises his eyebrows, "Laugh it up, Chuckles, you're taking it home."

———

Morning rain having passed, the rest of the day has been lovely. I gutted the fish and then cleaned up for work, although not well enough as I seem to smell the creature everywhere I go. The day is packed with study groups, meetings, and counselling sessions. I end my day at the hospital, visiting with two parishioners who will be there for about a week and a third who will not survive.

Elsie's already been in the hospital for over a month. Poked, prodded, and prescribed, the 89 year old spent her first few days in the ER waiting for a bed, before being transferred from one ward to another. The last time we visited, she was sleeping on a gurney in the hallway, waiting in line for another scan. When I asked her what message I could share with the congregation, she said, "Dearie, tell them that old Elsie's been sleeping around."

Memory failing and unable to retain names, she uses what she calls her dearie system. Instead of worrying about keeping track of everyone, she calls you "dearie," throws her arms out for a hug, and treats you like you're the most important person in her world.

The marvelous part is her ability to extend herself to each person who crosses her path without it becoming a matter of sacrifice. She's completely transparent about her needs, making her relationships absolutely reciprocal. There are times when I visit that she smiles, throws open her arms, and then says, "Dearie, I need to sleep. Can we do this another time?" or "Dearie, the coffee downstairs is better, would you take me to get a cup?" or "Dearie, I'm not looking for a minister right now. Can you be a normal person?"

As Elsie's abilities diminished, causing her world to become smaller, she shifted her expectations and celebrated attainable victories. She once described a trip to the washroom with a level of vivid detail usually reserved for recounting African safaris. At one point in the telling, she paused to catch her breath because she was laughing so hard. She referred to herself as a classic car, constantly in need of carburetor adjustment, plug cleaning, and filter changing – but beautiful to behold.

Which makes it all the more difficult to see her lying in bed today, clearly having taken a turn for the worse. Although her eyes are open, she doesn't notice me until I'm fully beside her bed. Turning her head, she lifts her arms slightly. Though she can't fully return the gesture, I give her a soft hug and kiss her cheek. There will be no recounting of adventures today. Sitting beside her and holding her hand, I begin to ramble on with news from the congregation and greetings from her friends. Without looking at me, she slowly raises her other hand, bringing a finger to her lips, signaling me to stop. Same Elsie. Because she keeps a firm grip of my hand, I know that I'm supposed to stay.

After a few minutes, she closes her eyes. I wait with her.

Simon leaves the hospital and heads toward home. The air is crisp and clear, persuading him to take a longer route. Approaching the park, he notices a few young people holding signs. He assumes protesters, until the behavior of passers-by suggests otherwise. Getting closer, he sees that the signs declare,

FREE HUGS

He slows, not to avoid, but to observe. Some people smile, but otherwise ignore the offer. A surprising number accept the hugs. Phones are pulled out. Pictures taken. Smiles shared.

Simon's distracted by a series of lively hugs at the other end of the group before he realizes that he's within range. A young woman bids, "Would you like a hug?"

"What's the cause?" he asks.

"No cause, except offering hugs," she responds with a lightness that comes from repetition.

"Why not?" Simon accepts.

The hug is lovely. Simon signals his release quickly, not wanting to overstay the welcome. No sooner does he say thanks than another member of the group, a young man, stretches out his arms. Simon makes his way down the line of seven, sharing hugs with them all. The dreadlocked woman at the end declares that he's an excellent hugger and asks him whether he'd like to hold the sign a while.

Simon shakes his head and says that he needs to get home, but the woman cajoles.

Holding up the sign, he watches the first few people walk past. Awkward. Then a group of friends in their thirties strides along and he hugs them all. A few more people decline before a man jumps off his bike for a quick fix. People in a car honk and wave. Simon feels himself tense at the approach of a street person, but he talks himself down by the time it's his turn to offer a hug. The man smells of alcohol and body odor. When he says, "Thanks, man, it's been a while," Simon feels like he's stumbled onto something unexpectedly wondrous. Fifteen minutes later, he relinquishes the sign to a new person.

Crossing the street to continue his journey home, Simon makes it as far as the first bench. There sits a man, perhaps in his late twenties. His arms bear a series of Celtic knots. Though not Simon's preference, the sleeves are remarkable pieces of art.

"What I enjoy…" the man pauses, aggressively chewing his gum, "what I enjoy is seeing how even the people who don't accept a hug react. A while ago there was this mother and toddler. They didn't take up the group on their offer, but as soon as they were past the hug zone, the kid wrapped herself around the mom's legs. If you watch you'll notice that some of the friends exchange one more hug on the next block." He continues to munch.

"You should give it a try," Simon offers.

"I was over there earlier. People sometimes hesitate when a guy with tats offers a hug, but they still brought me into the game. Pretty awesome." He blows a bubble. "Better than an average night at the pub."

"Not my usual either."

"You know," the young man pulls back the bubble and chews, "I've been watching now for two hours. You're the only person over 50 that's taken them up on their offer to hold a sign. I wonder why that is."

"Are you wondering why I took the sign or are you wondering why others don't?"

"Oh, I'm pretty clear about you. I'm concerned about the others. Of course, they might reach out in other ways, but sometimes people get stuck as they age. It's a drag." Another bubble.

Meeting like this is the icing on Simon's day. "Let me guess. You have a story that relates to this?"

Stops chewing. "Not really. Can't I wonder about something without having to tell a story about it? Besides, I'd rather celebrate. A lot of people are collecting their hugs and you faithfully represented your demographic. Did you see her delight when you accepted the sign?" They both look across the street at the group.

"Actually, I was more focused on questioning my decision."

The man turns to Simon, "Maybe so, but you've come a long way, my friend."

"I've had a lot of help and some distance to go."

"Again," he shakes his head and resumes chewing, "Just accept the bloody compliment."

It's Simon's turn to shake his head, "Thanks."

"Better," the young man smiles. "Now it happens that I do have a story about how far you can go with this."

"I'd be disappointed if you didn't."

―

Back when civil wars rocked feudal Japan, invading armies struck terror as they stormed into towns. Some villagers were forced into service, others killed outright. Buildings and fields representing generations of work were set to ruin in the space of a day.

Which is why the people of this particular village fell into panic when a rider galloped through town, warning of an approaching force.

Now meeting at the central square, they quickly agree that those too elderly to fight should take the children from the village and go into hiding. At all cost, the youngest needed to be kept safe. The rest would remain to face the army.

Having arrived late because of her slow pace, the old Nun from the temple asks the people how they plan to fight. In response, the villagers show her the weapons they've assembled.

The old woman takes one of the spears in her hand, comments on its fine quality and weight. She asks how many of them are trained in its use. No one steps forward.

She knows in her heart that the army will cut through them as easily as if they were a stand of young bamboo. "In your willingness to fight, you display great courage. At the same time, you will not triumph in the face of their experience. These men have spent their lives practicing the art of war. All of you must leave with the children and the elderly."

The people protest that if no one stays to protect the village, the army will take what it wants and set fire to the rest.

Signaling for the people to settle, the Nun offers, "I will stay and do my best to prevent this from happening."

Thanking the old woman for her wisdom, but placing little hope in her success, the villagers flee as quickly as possible, making their way into the hills before the arrival of the army.

Sitting on the mat of the open porch in front of the temple, the Nun sets out two cups and a pot. She waits.

The village fills with the sound of thundering hoofs before the horses come into sight. The troops are disciplined, entering homes to ensure that the occupants aren't waiting in ambush. The pillaging won't begin until the town is secure. It's not long before the old woman is discovered.

Word reaches the General that the people have fled, but an old Nun remains. Intrigued, he makes his way to the temple.

As the General approaches, the Nun shows no sign of submission. Instead, seated, she pours tea. The old woman's lack of concern irritates the General, who'd become accustomed to inciting fear. With measured reserve, he tips over the Nun's cups and pot, one at a time, with his foot. The woman slowly rises. Facing each other, the younger towers over the older.

The General asks, "Are you going to fight me on behalf of your village, old Nun?"

"If it is the only way to save my people," she replies.

Drawing his sword, the General says, "Then you should get your weapon."

"I won't be needing a weapon. I do not intend to harm anyone."

"Then how will you prove yourself stronger than me?"

"You will decide," the Nun calmly replies.

"Are you mocking me?" the General's temper soars. "Don't you realize that you are standing before a man who could run you through without blinking an eye?!"

The Nun allows but a moment before replying in a still voice, "General, do you not realize that you are standing before a woman who can be run through without blinking an eye?"

Raising his sword, the General sees that the old woman does not flinch. Knowing that if the roles were reversed, he would not do the same, he recognizes the superior strength of the Nun in this unusual battle. The General orders his army to depart, leaving the village intact. As he's about to leave the temple grounds, he stops in his tracks, faces the Nun, and bows.

The people return to find the old Nun sitting on the mat of the open porch, sipping freshly brewed tea.

Still elevated by the hugs and not particularly interested in being serious, I can't help myself, "Yah, the invading army thing. That happens a lot around here."

My companion bursts his newly formed bubble and laughs, "You used to be more staid."

"I used to be a lot of things," I muse. "Life's too short for most of them, and hardly long enough for the rest."

"So aside from comic relief, what did you notice about your reaction to the story?"

"All work and no play, eh?" I shift gears, "Though the nun seems ill-equipped for the circumstance, she's exactly what's needed. The other options would have led to destruction and/or bloodshed." I nod. "And she does it by being true to the life she built for herself. That life was more important than her own life, if you get what I mean. It's like life with a capital *L* versus life with a small *l*. Capital *L* life is about meaning and purpose. Small *l* life is about breathing another day. In the end, the former far outweighs the latter and the nun embodies that reality."

Raising an inked arm to point across the street, "Pretty easy to remember when people are offering hugs. Not so easy when an army's at your door."

"Sure, and that's what makes the daily gestures so important – like Elsie's approach right to her end. Those gestures remind us of what we can experience. When we're intentional about seeking out and offering those moments, we're better prepared for challenges to that way of being. It wasn't the nun's first day in the temple. She was a master. The moment with the general wasn't her first intentional act. It was the culmination of years of practice."

My friend's chewing slows. He delves, "How do you think the nun felt afterwards?"

I pause because my reflection isn't what I expect. My knee jerk response is "relief" and I then I think "pride" or "joy," but imagining her sitting on the open porch, drinking tea – none of these emotions fit.

"She feels at peace," I decide.

We fall into silence and watch the group across the street disband for the evening. Each of the members would have their own lives with their own fears and misgivings and their own hopes and joys. In the midst of it all, they tend their practice in this temple of their making. After offering hugs to so many others, the last set they share between themselves.

CHAPTER FIFTEEN

Bracing against the cold, I search for my destination in the distance.

When possible, I meet people on their own turf because of the insight it provides into their lives. Whether a house or a hospital room – the pictures and cards on display, the reading material beside the chair, the content being channeled through radio or television or laptop, the beverage offered, the signs of other people's comings and goings – all speak volumes.

And they seldom mislead.

We can say or think anything about ourselves, but our artifacts offer a more objective portrayal. The origin of items, the memories they evoke, these point to our journeys. The chandelier that seems out of place but was once an anniversary gift between grandparents. The unusual painting received as a token of appreciation. The houseplant that started as a cutting from one friend and has since proliferated into the homes of others.

Checking another street sign, I realize that I'm skirting Frank's neighborhood. When it came to artifacts, his bedside table spoke to me like no other. It was our first meeting and no fewer than ten books were piled at his side. In no discernably rational order, classic volumes like Frankl's *Man's Search for Meaning*, and Reps/Senzaki's *Zen Flesh, Zen Bones,* and Schama's *The Story of the Jews* were piled on top of Larson's *Far Side Gallery 4*. The correlation between the stack and the workings of his mind were unmistakable. Add the Guinness infused cheese and all was made clear.

The memory of the stack rouses delight; an involuntary puff of laughter clouds the cold before my face. Amazed by how the short relationship has stayed with me, I walk the final blocks in his company, my touchstone for matters philosophical and waggish.

It's unlikely that the coffee house down this street will afford such specific clues about the internal workings of the young man I'm meeting. In fact, to this point all of my contact with him has unfolded outside of his home. My first meeting was at the funeral home. Because my schedule was tight, the next had to be in my office. Then there was the service itself.

For this day's gathering, I suggested his place, but the man was adamant that we meet in a coffee shop. I let him choose the location, which proved to be a bit more of a walk than expected. The dark sky threatens precipitation, but whether it falls as rain or snow is anyone's guess.

Arriving at the door, I note that the place is packed – a good sign, providing we can find a seat.

―――

Simon casually surveys the room while his companion retrieves their coffees. The cracked plaster walls are augmented by elegantly framed vinyl record covers, mostly from progressive rock groups of the 70s and 80s, though one corner is devoted to punk icons. On a sideboard, a turntable is open for public use. Beside and below, milk crates hold a vast selection of LPs. Although clients select the music, the volume remains at the staff's discretion via an integrated amp behind the till. Given the current decibel level, they approve of Jethro Tull.

The clientele is surprisingly mixed. Some were in high school when the albums were released. Others have aligned their 15-year-old identities to another generation's work. Looking at the crowd, it's easy to speculate that they passed five Starbucks on the way to this coffee shop. It's a destination.

Which leads Simon to tentatively draw a few conclusions about his new companion, who weaves his way back to their table. Though he's barely into his twenties, his parents were buried a few months ago, victims of a head-on collision with a texting truck driver. Usually people don't accept Simon's offer for follow-up conversations, unless there's a prior relationship. This time's different. As the young man sets down the drinks, Simon notices a worn wedding band on the ring finger of his right hand, perhaps his father's. His black t-shirt is vintage Clash. Up until now, Simon has only seen him in suit and tie.

"It's been a tough couple of months," he admits. "I miss my folks. Didn't realize how much of my life still centered on them."

"Tell me," Simon encourages.

"You think that you're an adult, right. That you want them in your life because you love them and not because you need them. And then it all goes to hell and you find out that you still liked having a mom and a dad. I was sick in bed for a couple days last month and I didn't know how to make mom's 'sickie' broth. When my bike chain snapped the next week, I tried to text my dad for a ride."

"What happened when it didn't connect?"

"I started to tear up," he sighs before smiling at himself, "and then I walked a long way."

Simon joins in the smile, "It's not easy, the grieving. What else have you noticed?"

"Some days I have to drag myself out of bed. When friends call, I go, but I don't feel like going."

"Do you always go out when they ask?"

"No," he responds, "sometimes I bow out, but then I feel like I've let them down."

"What would they tell you?" Simon asks.

"To not be stupid," he offers.

"You have good friends."

He smiles, nods, and takes a long drink from his cup, "They're wonderful."

Simon speculates, "They're wonderful and…?"

"They're wonderful and they don't get what's going on for me. It's completely outside their worlds. Most of them haven't experienced the death of a grandparent, let alone a parent. Both of mine are gone."

"How can I help?"

The young man contemplates his coffee before taking another drink, "Up until now, life's been pretty straight forward. Reasonably great childhood. Okay marks in school. No dark secrets. No medical crises. I was plodding along happily enough." Another sip. "With my folks dying, it's changed. Life feels kind of meaningless. Like, what's the point? Here one day and gone the next." He picks up his cup, brings it to his lips, then starts to talk again before drinking, "Then I take a look around after the funeral and everyone else is getting on with their lives, so I realize that the problem isn't so much with life; it's me. I'm the one lacking purpose." He finally takes a gulp and swallows. "Do you get what I mean?"

Simon readies himself to offer a response, but takes a different tack. "Tell you what. I'm going to ask you to go out on a limb with me." Simon leans forward, "Let me share an old story and see if it speaks to your situation." He reads uncertainty in the young man's eyes, "Sounds crazy, I know, but you might be surprised. Given that this is your coffee shop, you're not looking for an ordinary path. Shall we try it once, no obligation to continue?"

The young man takes a read of Simon's face, "Go for it."

―――

There once was a wealthy Prince out on the hunt with his companions. They stay out beyond their usual time, tracking a deer far into the forest. Caught up in the chase, they don't notice the clouds gathering until the storm is upon them. The first flash of lightning thunders directly over their heads without warning, spooking their horses. The Prince gets separated from the rest as his horse plunges deeper into the forest. When he tries to steady the animal, it rears, throwing him to the ground. As the deluge soaks through his layers of clothing, he watches his horse disappear into the woods.

Cold, wet, and miserable, the Prince rises to his feet and begins to walk in what he hopes is the right direction. Noticing sleet mixed in with the rain, he realizes that his life is in jeopardy. After a few hour's walk, his limbs grow heavy and his mind sleepy.

The Prince stumbles into a clearing and sees a cabin, windows lit.

Moments later, he's out of his wet clothes and wrapped in a warm blanket by a fire. An elderly couple bring him some wine. They listen to his tale with great interest and tell the Prince that he is not far from home, but it's not safe to travel in such a storm. The woman insists that he must stay with them for soup and a good night's rest. The Prince doesn't want to impose, but there is little choice.

Sitting around a table, the old couple extend their hands to each other and the Prince. They recite their prayers in a language he doesn't understand, but he's glad to be in their circle. More wine is poured, bread is served along with a delicious soup. The Prince declares that it's the best soup he's ever tasted, unparalleled in aroma, texture, and flavor.

Later, the woman pulls out a penny whistle and leads the men in familiar songs. At one point the old man starts to dance, but quickly descends into laughter at his elderly frame's disinclination to cooperate. The Prince feels renewed and their conversation goes late into the night before he enjoys a wonderfully sound sleep.

The next morning, they share breakfast together. The Prince has the old woman explain the recipe for the soup, which he records in minute detail. Saying his goodbyes and offering a promise of return, he thanks them for their hospitality and follows their directions home.

Upon his arrival, he calls for the Royal Chef and tells him about the incredibly delicious soup. He describes not only the vegetables, but how they were cut; not only the meat, but how it was braised. For each herb and seasoning, he notes the exact amount. Not knowing whether it makes a difference, he also details the pot, the fire, everything he can remember. He asks that the soup be prepared for dinner that evening.

The Prince chuckles at his own impatience for the meal to begin. He heads down to the dining hall and sits before a large, crackling fire. The soup is presented in a fine china bowl. With a deep breath, he takes in the aroma before dipping his spoon into the surface. He blows across the spoonful and then tastes the soup. It's good. Perhaps, very good. But it isn't as good as the old woman's soup.

Disappointed, he calls for the Royal Chef, who insists that every detail was followed, right down to the shape of the pot in which it was cooked. Not convinced, the Prince goes with the Chef to the kitchen and oversees a second attempt to get it right. The result is the same. It's good soup, but not nearly as good as the night before.

The Prince doesn't doubt the intentions of the old woman, but she must have forgotten to mention an ingredient. The next morning he sets out for their house.

After a warm greeting and some conversation, the Prince comments again about the wonderful soup. The woman asks if he passed the recipe to his cooks. The Prince laughs and says that they weren't able to make it to the same superb level. Perhaps something was missing? After listening to him rattle off the ingredients, the old woman assures him that nothing was missed.

"But how can that be?" he asks. "There must be some special way that you prepare the soup."

The man and woman look at each other, sharing a smile. "I think," the old man says, "that you have it backward."

"You entered our house cold and wet," the woman explains, "but soon you were warm and dry."

"In the storm you were afraid and alone," the man continues, "but with us you were safe among friends."

"You see," beams the woman, "the soup was not prepared in a special way for you. You were prepared in a special way for the soup."

The Prince nods his head in silence as the words sink into place. He understands. After more conversation about the events of their lives, he thanks the old couple for their hospitality, and takes his leave. Over time, he becomes a regular visitor to their home and they to his.

I look for a reaction from my young companion. He's not saying anything. Maybe this was a crazy idea. What was I thinking? Okay, slow down. Ask a question.

"So what did you notice about your response to the story?" I try to sound confident. The words feel cut and pasted.

It's all he needs, "Yah, I connect with the Prince being lost in the woods. That's totally where I'm at right now – and it would be great to find that cabin." He pauses, "But more than that, I relate to the bit about what makes the soup special. Like I said, at first when my folks died it was like life had lost its meaning, until I realized that everyone else was moving on with theirs. Then I figured out that it's my sense of purpose that got lost. That's sort of like the soup. It's not that life is going to change so that it's meaningful for me. I need to do the work so that I find my purpose in life. At least, that's what came to mind. Did I get it right?"

I'm relieved and surprised, elated even. "The great thing about these stories is that it's not a matter of there being a right answer. All they do is offer new ways to frame what's going on for us."

"Look," my companion checks his phone, "I'd like to talk more, but I have to go, sorry. I'm wondering if we can meet again. Maybe you can coach me through the purpose question, if that's okay for you. I get the feeling that you're not going to provide answers, which I appreciate, but

I do need a guide. And you're right about my preference for different paths."

I'm delighted. "Get to your next appointment and I'll send you a couple of times when I'm available next week. See you then."

We stand. I extend my hand and receive a hug.

———

After the young man leaves, Simon sits back down to finish the last of his cappuccino.

Someone takes the seat across from him. "Can I help you?" he asks.

"Come on, aren't you at least going to give me some credit?" she responds.

The woman is somewhere in her forties. Large, stunning brown eyes. She wears a form fitting khaki shirt and jeans. Bright yellow lettering spells out M*A*S*H 4077th.

"Eavesdropping?"

She feigns distress, "Must you make it sound rude?" She grins and shifts tone, "You did good by that kid."

"Thank you."

"And you're willing to receive a compliment without argument. This is a golden day."

He laughs, "Given enough chances, growth is possible."

"Speaking of growth, I'm stealing your story and adding it my collection," she proclaims.

"Not my story, so go ahead. Do you want to stay here or shall we walk?"

Large flakes of snow descend from the sky, swirling with the slight wind. Her leather jacket defends her from the cold. Simon's oilskin coat shows obvious signs of wear and welcomes the icy breeze through every seam. Still, he walks without reservation.

Although they are side-by-side, she picks the direction. They end up on Frank's street by the benches where they sat shortly before his death. Brushing off the thin layer of snow, they brave the cold, watching the snow accumulate on the trees like a layer of blossoms. The pavement gradually moves through the grey scale on its way to becoming white.

"I remember when you first visited me," Simon recalls. "You told me to stop editing other people's stories and figure out whether mine's worth telling."

Her voice is matter-of-fact, "You did deserve a kick."

"And then you hassled me for making assumptions about people. And next you got me thinking about my own funeral."

She looks at him, "You sound angry."

"That's the cold," he shudders. "I feel grateful."

"How so?"

"You helped me find my life when I didn't know that I had lost it, especially Ailish. The last time we sat here — the whole bit about 'this, too, shall pass' — those stories were a lifeline."

"Not so much because of me, then, but the stories."

Simon grins, "So I'm told."

"Touché. What else made a difference?"

He absent-mindedly shifts snow around with his shoe, creating a small pile between his feet, "The people who died. Even the ones I don't want to emulate made my path clearer. Then you add on the Arjuns and Louises and Elsies and Franks. Talk about inspiration."

She reminds him, "But in the end the work is yours."

"If I want an exceptional meal," he winks, "I need to prepare myself for the soup."

They watch the snow accumulate in silence. When she eventually stands, he joins her. As she reaches across and holds his hand between hers, he senses her reluctance to say goodbye. It both surprises him and not. Before she speaks, Simon touches her cheek and nods, "I know."

More snow falls.

"You better get going before one of us freezes," he continues. "I'd say that I'm looking forward to seeing you again, but I might not be so enthusiastic when the day comes." He embraces her in a hug, "Take care, my friend."

My pace quickens, but only because of the cold. I'm looking forward to a warm shower before joining friends this evening. Snow that started as a flurry falls more earnestly. The blanket transforms every surface, quieting the cars as they roll past. It starts to squeak beneath my feet.

Vividly, a memory from the past takes me back. Ailish was five or six years old at most. My wife had started a new job at the university. I took the day off and snuck up to campus with Ailish. We built a snowman beneath her second story office window. Sticks for arms. Rocks for eyes, mouth, and buttons. Carrot for nose. Once we finished, we broke into a snowball fight, covering each other in white.

I found out later that my wife didn't notice at first. Her colleagues were gathered at the window, commenting on the father and daughter playing in the snow, how adorable it was. Only after a while did she look out and see what the fuss was about. She left her desk and joined us.

One of the most perfect moments of my life.

And not the last.

APPENDIX:
SOURCES FOR THE WISDOM STORIES

I confess that I'm happy to tell a good story, even when I'm unsure of its origin. As long as I let others know that it's not my own work, I'm satisfied.

None of the wisdom stories contained in this book are my creations. I may have embellished details, lengthened narratives, altered genders, perhaps even shifted emphasis to suit my purposes, but their beginnings are not by my hand. Some are ancient tales, others relatively modern. A handful attest clear provenances; others are in dispute. A few are so common across a number of cultures that it seems unfair to favor one source over another. Sadly, a couple have been separated from any trace of their origins, even though they're easily accessible on the web.

To the best of my ability, I offer these words of context. Hopefully they'll provide a starting point for those who wish to dig deeper into the tales, along with the traditions that first gave them voice.

Chapter One – Maybe, Maybe Not

Clear examples of this global story can be found in Jewish, Taoist, and Buddhist collections. One popular version set in China tells of a man's run-away horse, which initiates a series of losses and gains that eventually save his son from being forced into battle by the local warlord. In the wonderful anthology of Jewish Folktales, *Solomon and the Ant*, Sheldon Oberman and Peninnah Schram connect their version through the Babylonian Talmud to Rabbi Akiva's life and teaching (50-135 C.E.).

Chapter Two – Value of a Ring

Quite opposite to the previous tale, I've only been able to find unattributed versions of this story posted throughout the Internet (stories.reachoutblogs.com). I confess that I added the final movement, which both recognizes the input of others and leaves the determination of the ring's ultimate value to its owner.

Chapter Three – The Matriarch and the Wine

My version builds on elements contained in two separate stories. Several renditions of "The Pond of Milk" suggest that the tale's origins are Islamic (islamcan.com). Similar in theme, "The Communal Wine," centers on a tribal people deep in a jungle (stories-of-wisdom.com). Neither provide definitive word on origins.

Chapter Four – Ox and Monkey

This selection is reworked from a collection of Buddhist Jataka tales retold by Mark McGinnis in *Buddhist Animal Wisdom Stories*, which in turn drew from a late 19th Century collection by E.B. Cromwell, which found its source in the Pali Buddhist scriptures, which are some of the earliest Buddhist texts dating to the 4th Century BCE. The Jataka tales recount the prior incarnations of the Buddha.

Chapter Five – Two Wolves

My favorite story behind a story, "Two Wolves" is hotly debated. On many websites, including those of First Nations groups, the origin is stated as Cherokee. The claim is contested by other groups, some of whom assert that the story was adapted from a 1978 book by famed evangelist Billy Graham. At least we can say that the story is likely of North American origin.

Chapter Six – The Worst Poison

According to Oberman and Schram, the hero of this tale is Moses Ben Maimon (1135-1204 C.E.), a famed Jewish scholar. Living in Spain and Egypt, Maimon is said to have not only mastered medicine, but also law, philosophy, religion, and astronomy.

Chapter Seven – Story of the Talents

This confusing and insightful parable of Jesus can be found in Matthew 25:14-30. Biblical scholars will be familiar with the various frustrations offered by Simon, which represent only a portion of the ongoing discussion.

Chapter Eight – The Woman and the Pail

A version of this tale has come to be broadly identified as part of the collections of the teachings, stories, and sayings of Mohammad, known as the Hadith. However, some sources note that the tale doesn't reflect content found in the actual Hadith. Still others claim that the story was adapted from one concerning the founder of the Baha'i faith, Baha'u'llah. Authenticating this counter claim is yet another challenge. That members of two traditions wish to claim the same story speaks to its power, but unfortunately not its ultimate origin.

Chapter Nine – The Master and the River

Written by the Taoist philosopher Zhuang Zhou, who lived during the late 4th and early 3rd Centuries BCE, this tale can be found in *Zhuangzi*. In the original version, Kong Qiu (Confucius) watches an old man struggle against the current. I first read the story in Benjamin Hoff's very accessible work, *The Tao of Pooh*.

Chapter Ten – The Ring of Wisdom

One of the numerous legends attached to Solomon, this tale involves his most faithful servant, Benaiah. This version is closer to the one found in *Solomon and the Ant* than other accounts which have Solomon taking pleasure in sending his servant on an impossible errand. Similar themes are pursued in Zen Buddhist stories, using the line "It will pass." A North African version follows the fortunes of a man who is free, then sold into slavery, until eventually he inherits his master's riches, before turning ill.

Chapter Eleven – The Young Archer

Although a much shorter form of this story is posted widely across the Internet (spiritualminds.com), I have yet to find one that names the source for this tale. Whether ancient or modern, at least there appears to be little argument that it has earned a place within the Buddhist tradition.

Chapter Thirteen – The Abbot and the Rabbi

The original form of this story was published in 1979 by Francis Dorff in *New Catholic World* under the title, "The Rabbi's Gift." An astounding statement on the value of reaching out to other traditions as a way of understanding one's own, I first came across the work in William Bausch's *A World of Stories*. I extend my appreciation to Father Dorff, who generously extended his permission for me to use an adaptation of the story for this book.

Chapter Fourteen – The Nun and the General

Much like "The Young Archer," a short version of this tale seems to be a part of every second Buddhist story collection, none of which seem to disclose source information (viewonbuddhism.org).

Chapter Fifteen – The Taste of Soup

Adapted from another Jewish folktale, this Talmudic legend connects the Roman Emperor Antonius to Rabbi Judah ha-Nasi. The story's original focus was on the difference made by the Sabbath. Although widely shared, a version can be found in *Solomon and the Ant*.

ABOUT THE AUTHOR

Currently serving as the Chaplain and Faculty Mentor at St. Michaels University School, Keven divides his time between public speaking, process facilitation, and exploring life choices with staff and students. An ordained minister within the United Church of Canada, his roles centered on congregational ministry and conflict resolution support. Prior to this work, Keven joined an organizational change and development firm, specialising in values identification and organizational culture within both the private and public sectors. Alongside these endeavors, Keven headed a non-profit that promoted discussion on ethics within the corporate community, including the establishment of a regional ethics award in conjunction with the country's largest credit union. Keven also served on the boards of outreach societies that focused on providing food, shelter, and services to members of the street community.

When It Matters Most reflects a distillation of all these roles.

The book's core rests on a series of traditional wisdom tales that Keven learned while preparing messages for his 1000 strong community. Wanting to bring the globally diverse stories to a wider audience,

Keven wrapped a narrative around the tales, connected to the life of a disaffected minister. To illustrate the veracity of the wisdom, the novel focuses on the emotional and spiritual complexities of death as a way to shed light on how we choose to live. Drawing on his direct experience with the dying and their families, along with his time in corporate board rooms and homeless shelters, Keven creates an ensemble of characters that represents the span of the human condition.

In his career, Keven has spoken at gatherings ranging from professional associations and education symposiums to circles of kindergarten students. His current community represents twenty-five countries and five continents. Given the requirements of his role, writing and speaking are a constant part of his life, including contributions of non-fiction work within his field.

Holding degrees in Economics (Bachelor of Arts) and Theology (Master of Divinity and Master of Theology), Keven's formal academic focus was on Applied Ethics and Corporate Culture. Afterwards, his learning interests expanded to include Mediation, Conflict Resolution, Leadership Theory, Character Education and Professional/Personal Coaching.

Keven lives in Victoria, British Columbia with his amazingly resilient wife of over 25 years. Their daughter is currently completing her Master's in Ireland, causing him moments of intense jealousy. Over the years, the household has included a series of cats, several Great Danes, and, almost inexplicably, one Miniature Schnauzer. When not speaking or deep in conversation, Keven can be found commuting on his bike, playing with his camera, or enjoying great food with friends.

You can connect with Keven through kevenfletcher.com, @kevenfletcher, or Elevate Publishing.

A strategic publisher empowering authors to strengthen their brand.

Visit Elevate Publishing for our latest offerings.
www.elevatepub.com

NO TREES WERE HARMED IN THE MAKING OF THIS BOOK

OK, so a few did need to make the ultimate sacrifice.

In order to steward our environment, we are partnering with *Plant With Purpose*, to plant a tree for every tree that paid the price for the printing of this book.

⇒ PLANT WITH PURPOSE
www.plantwithpurpose.org

go to www.elevatepub.com/about to learn more